"I'm attracted to you," Jake said finally

He watched Torey with hooded eyes. "And you're afraid of me."

"I am not."

He looked skeptical. "You've been running in the other direction since you got off that plane. Why? You used to want me."

"That was years ago," Torey stammered. "I was a stupid, innocent child."

"And now you're a big, brave woman," Jake said sarcastically. "So why are you running away?"

"Did it ever occur to your conceited ego that I might have learned something in the past seven years? I met Paul and found out what true love really is. And what it's not." She flung her braid back indignantly and turned toward the kitchen door. "And I have no intention of settling for less the second time around!"

Books by Anne McAllister

HARLEQUIN PRESENTS
844 – LIGHTNING STORM

HARLEQUIN ROMANCE
2721 – DARE TO TRUST

HARLEQUIN AMERICAN ROMANCE
89 – STARSTRUCK
108 – QUICKSILVER SEASON

These books may be available at your local bookseller.

Don't miss any of our special offers. Write to us at the following address for information on our newest releases.

Harlequin Reader Service
P.O. Box 52040, Phoenix, AZ 85072-2040
Canadian address: P.O. Box 2800, Postal Station A,
5170 Yonge St., Willowdale, Ont. M2N 6J3

ANNE McALLISTER

lightning storm

Harlequin Books

TORONTO • NEW YORK • LONDON
AMSTERDAM • PARIS • SYDNEY • HAMBURG
STOCKHOLM • ATHENS • TOKYO • MILAN

To Nikki, for instigation, and to Dan, for inspiration

Harlequin Presents first edition December 1985
ISBN 0-373-10844-3

Original hardcover edition published in 1985
by Mills & Boon Limited

CHAPTER ONE

'GOOD grief, Torey,' her sister groaned as she heaved the bulging suitcase on to the baggage conveyor belt. 'This thing weighs a ton! What did Mom stick into it besides her last minute bag of cookies?'

Torey Cooper grinned, tossing her long black plait over her shoulder, 'A man probably. When I went back inside to pat the dog goodbye, she probably opened it and stuffed Vince Liebfried inside.'

'Or Harlan Nelson,' Debbie said. 'Disguised as a bag of double chocolate chip mounds.' She giggled in her reference to Harlan's obvious corpulence, then stepped back and waited while Torey checked in for her flight from Chicago's O'Hare Airport to Los Angeles. 'You know, Torey,' she went on seriously when her sister finally rejoined her, 'Mom does mean well.'

Torey sighed. 'Of course she does. But subtlety isn't in Mother's vocabulary. Or in anyone else's in the family either. Even Paul's folks were starting to screen the eligible men for me. They sent me an unattached spot welder from Dubuque when the loader broke, and last week they invited me over for Sunday dinner and just happened to arrange for the new minister to be there too. The new *single* minister! And the man Dad sent out to look over the dairy herd spent more time talking about local night spots than he did about milk yield. It's been getting so that I never know if the fertiliser dealer is there for me or the manure!'

Debbie laughed at the pained expression on her sister's face. 'But you know they're only trying to help,' she protested. 'They just don't want you to go on mourning Paul forever.'

'I am not mourning Paul forever,' Torey snapped,

more irritably than she would have wished. 'Paul was my husband, for heaven's sake. Even though he's been dead for two years and I don't weep every day of my life anymore, I still love him and I still miss him. And I shall probably go on missing him for a very long time. There aren't many men like Paul around, and I don't intend replacing him just to have a man—any man!'

'Nobody's suggesting that,' Debbie protested, trailing behind Torey as she sailed through the crowds of people heading for the boarding area.

'In this case, actions speak louder than words,' Torey grumbled. 'Every time I turned around I was falling over somebody's brother-in-law or second cousin. And they're not remotely interesting. Not one of them.'

'You were spoiled,' Debbie argued. 'Paul is a hard act to follow.'

'He is,' Torey agreed. Her green eyes got a faraway look in them which meant that she wasn't seeing the airport anymore, but rather a craggy face with warm brown eyes, copper hair and a ruddy farmer's tan. What they had had together was so special that she had no patience with her family's matchmaking attempts. 'Which is why,' she said firmly to her sister, 'I am glad to escape. If ever there was a fortuitous event, Gran's knee surgery is it.'

'Gran wouldn't thank you for saying so,' Debbie laughed.

'Probably not. But you have to admit, it was lucky for me. I'd got the farm sold and I was still job hunting. Anyway, who could possibly be better qualified to care for her than an unemployed physiotherapist?' Even if she hadn't practised as a therapist since she and Paul had been out on the farm, she still knew her business and, in fact, it would be a good reintroduction into the field. She hoped someone would consider her grandmother a good job reference.

'Who indeed?' Debbie agreed. 'Besides,' she teased, 'who knows? You might be playing right into Mom's hands. After all, there are bound to be more eligible bachelors per square inch in southern California than in northern Illinois.'

'No fear,' Torey said firmly. 'California is life in the fast lane, remember? Who's going to take the time to look at a little old lady tractor driver like me?'

Debbie rolled her eyes. 'You are only twenty-five,' she argued. 'And Vince and Harlan sure look at you.'

'That's only because I'm a diversion from seed catalogues and soybean plants,' Torey replied, dismissing the only two single farmers in the area. 'Besides, they mean nothing to me. And all southern California has is more Vinces and Harlans—with one difference. The ones in California left their common sense out east.'

'What do you mean?'

Torey shook her head, remembering the summer seven years ago that she had spent with her grandparents in California. To a naïve eighteen year old it had proved to be a painfully enlightening experience. 'Never mind,' she said. 'You don't want to know. Suffice to say that men like Paul aren't thick on the ground.' She had never told Debbie about the man she'd had eyes for that summer, and she wasn't going to start now.

The loudspeaker crackled and announced the boarding call for Torey's flight. She felt a welling of emotion as her sister hugged her impulsively. 'Time to go, I guess,' she said, a trifle shaky now that the moment was at hand.

'Say hi to Gran,' Debbie said. 'Be good.' Her eyes twinkled. 'But don't feel you have to confine yourself to doing only what I would do!'

'I won't,' Torey grinned. 'But don't expect anything. I mean, I'm not going to be bringing home Mr California.'

'What? No surfers?' Debbie teased.

Torey made a face. 'No, thanks. Not for me.' She

gave Debbie a final peck on the cheek and an extra squeeze. 'Thanks so much for bringing me, Deb. Tell Don I appreciate the loan of his wife for the day. I'm glad you could bring me.' Tears pricked her eyes and she blinked rapidly and managed a watery smile. 'Hug that little niece of mine for me.' She turned then and bolted up the indoor gangway to the plane, a sudden crush of faces and memories plaguing her, assaulting her with might-have-beens. And as she sank wearily into her window seat she thought for the first time in several months, Oh Paul, why you? Why me?

Stop being maudlin, she told herself. The time for post-mortems had come and gone. She could no longer allow herself to indulge in thinking about what might have been if only Paul had gone to town that day instead of out into the field, if only the recent rains hadn't caused more erosion than usual, if only his tractor hadn't tipped . . . She closed her eyes and leant back, feeling the throb of the jet engines right up through the back of the seat into her head.

'Something to drink, miss?' the flight attendant asked once they were underway. Torey glanced at her seatmate, a hardworking businessman from the look of his overflowing briefcase. He was having a scotch on the rocks, and though generally Torey would have asked for a soft drink, she thought she could use something a little stronger at the moment. But not a scotch, which would likely have her flat out in the aisle after three sips.

'White wine?' she asked, and the steward nodded and poured her a glass. Torey took a tentative sip thinking wryly that at nine-thirty in the morning her mother was probably hanging out the laundry and would doubtless think her older daughter was completely decadent to be sipping wine over Iowa at 33,000 feet.

But that's *my* choice, Torey thought and reflected that, in a way, 'choice' was what this whole escape to California was all about. If she had stayed in Galena any longer she wouldn't have had a choice of her own left to make. There were far too many parents, brothers, sisters, aunts, uncles, cousins and in-laws in the small Illinois town who were only too willing to make every decision for her. All her available energy recently had been spent trying to convince them not to!

In their opinion, without Paul, Torey was lost, adrift—and it was their duty to take care of her, find her a job, an apartment, and—eventually—a man. It would have been funny if it hadn't been so real, Torey thought, remembering how their machinations some-times bordered on the absurd. She finished her wine and lay back, closing her eyes, hoping as she did so that when she unpacked her suitcase this afternoon she wouldn't really find Vince Liebfried inside.

Naps were wonderful, she decided when she opened her eyes an hour later to discover that the glumness and the memories had receded. She sat up and dug into her scrambled eggs with surprising gusto, feeling a stirring of eagerness at the thought of seeing Gran again and of once more being a part of the land of palm trees and eight lane freeways, of bougainvillaea and sandy beaches. And what a pleasure it was to come back a woman, confident and self-assured, quite different from the gawky, naïve teenager who had descended on the land of the lotus-eaters once before. Her childlike pixie hair cut of long ago had grown for years into the long black tresses that now, unplaited, hung nearly to her waist. Her face, too, had matured, the wide green eyes and generous mouth no longer seeming too powerful but instead strikingly attractive. And if she no longer looked like the child who had come to California seven years ago, she no longer felt like her either. Her love for Paul and her marriage had given her a knowledge, a maturity, and a serenity that his death could never erase.

She broke off a piece of Danish pastry and buttered it, remembering with equal parts fondness and embarrassment, the innocent she had been. Well, there would be no more of that. She was immune to glitter now, to shallowness and to easy-come-easy-go relationships. With Paul she had had the real thing, an enduring love, and she wasn't settling for less. Debbie might be right about the number of bachelors in LA outnumbering the ones back home, but she didn't have to worry about them, Torey decided. They were only looking for one thing—a tumble in bed—and that wasn't what Torey wanted at all, any more than she had ever wanted it.

'Go home and grow up, kid.' She remembered the gruff voice as if it had been yesterday. It could still make her ears burn just thinking about it. But, she sighed, he had certainly been right. She had needed to grow up, though perhaps not in the way he had meant. He had thought she ought to develop a little sophistication before she dated any more swinging singles. But she had discovered very quickly that 'to swing' wasn't what she wanted at all. Anyway, it didn't matter any longer for she had found Paul again when she went home, and even though he was gone now, she had learned something. Surface attraction wasn't enough. She would never fall for it again. A slight smile played across her features as she thought of that young man of long ago. What would the mature Torey Cooper see in him? Not much, she speculated. Not after having known real love with Paul.

'Not long now,' the man in the next seat said to her as he began to shovel his papers back into his briefcase. He raked a weary hand through thinning hair. 'Good to get home, eh?'

'It's not my home,' Torey explained. 'I'm visiting my grandmother. She just had surgery.'

The man frowned. 'You being met?' he asked.

'Yes. Her tenant's picking me up. It's all arranged.'

'Good. Single gals shouldn't wander around here alone.'

Torey supposed he was right. 'Single gals' felt quite comfortable wandering around Galena and its environs alone, but perhaps large international airports were another matter. Gran had certainly seemed to think so. When Torey had written to tell her when she would be arriving, Gran had called her mother and demanded to know Torey's flight number, saying, 'Jake will pick her up.'

All Torey's protests about being an adult and independent were swept aside as so much straw. 'Why fiddle with a cab when you have a perfectly willing man to pick you up?' her mother had said, the emphasis on the word *man* being unintentional but obvious.

'Many cab drivers are *men*, Mother,' she had snapped, 'and who knows if this Jake is "perfectly willing"? Maybe no one asked him. You know Gran.'

But apparently Gran had, for word came back that Jake would be there, not to fear, and Torey, knowing when it wasn't worth arguing with her mother's set expression, gave up. She even had the grace to feel slightly childish after she grumbled, 'Tell him to wear a flower behind his ear so I'll recognise him,' as she flounced out of the room.

'He'll wear a red shirt,' her mother informed her the night before she left. 'Gran says that's enough.'

Torey grinned. 'If that's all he's wearing I'm sure that it will be!'

Her mother's face went brick red. 'Oh, Torey, you . . .' she spluttered. 'You know what I mean!'

Torey did, but she wondered after she had disembarked from the plane if her mother had any idea just how many men in southern California were wearing red shirts this particular Monday morning in June. She saw a sweaty construction worker in a grimy red tank top and low-slung blue jeans, an arty, flamboyant type in a flowing red silk shirt with billowing sleeves, and any number of middle-aged men in tomato red sports shirts and white duck pants or madras-patterned golf

slacks. Not one of them gave her a second glance.
Perhaps *she* should have worn the flower behind her
ear!

The crowds of people moved away to get their
luggage or to converse with those meeting them, and
Torey stood by the window, camel-coloured, light-
weight coat tossed over her arm, and surveyed the
scene. Not a promising red shirt in sight. Not a man of
any description looking her way. Amazing. She felt
immeasurably lighter. Maybe escape to California had
been the answer. For the first time in months she felt
free of measuring, calculating male eyes. Heaving a sigh
of relief she turned and watched the plane ease away
from the building and trundle down the runway to take
off.

'Excuse me.' The voice was low, familiar somehow,
and right behind her left ear. 'Are you Victoria
Cooper?'

She turned to say that she was, but her tongue was
suddenly immobilised. It couldn't be. But then she
realised that it couldn't *not* be. No two men had those
ice chip blue eyes, the heavy dark brows beneath
shaggy, equally dark hair. No two men could have that
uncompromising jaw, thin, aquiline nose, and sensual
mouth. She closed her eyes for a moment, grateful for
the window to lean back on.

'Are you all right?' He was staring at her, concerned,
and she realised that he didn't know her. The
astonished, white-faced woman he had come to meet
apparently bore no resemblance to the awkward
teenager he had known once before.

'F-fine,' she mumbled, and took a deep, cleansing
breath. 'Just a little unsteady after the plane trip, I
guess.' She heard a hollow little laugh that didn't sound
like hers at all but couldn't have come from anyone
else.

'You *are* Victoria Cooper? Mrs Harrison's granddaughter?' He was looking at her curiously, intently,

and she remembered how one glance from those eyes had made her melt seven years ago.

'Yes, I am,' she said, finally getting a grip on herself. It was just the shock of it, that was all, she told herself firmly. 'And you...' she allowed herself a sweeping gaze that covered him from the toes of his tattered jogging shoes past well-worn, snug blue jeans and a vivid red Jack Daniel's Whiskey T-shirt to settle on the once—beloved face, 'must be Jake.' She offered her hand, amazed at her coolness, pleased that she had, in fact, 'grown up'.

'Of the red shirt,' he grinned, then shrugged. 'I had to buy it specially.'

Torey smiled in spite of herself. 'You could have worn a flower in your ear,' she told him. 'I did suggest it.'

'I heard.' His voice was dry but his eyes were twinkling. 'I was afraid if I did I might look like everyone else.'

Torey didn't think there was much chance of that. He was every bit as compelling as he had ever been. Jake, if that was what his name was, would never get lost in a crowd. 'Jake what?' she asked now as she followed him down endless corridors towards the exit, Jake carrying her case.

'Brosnan.' He turned and slanted her a grin. 'James Patrick Brosnan at your service,' he said, pretending to doff an imaginary cap.

'Mmmm,' she mumbled, satisfied. J.B. was what he had been called seven years ago. There had been J.B. and Mick and Cliffie and Wicks—nicknames all, as though real names hadn't mattered, as though what happened on the beach had no relation to what happened in real life. Torey dropped back slightly, watching him move ahead of her, admiring as she had before the natural grace of the man. In water he had been a seal, on land a lean hungry cat with pale, icy eyes. I'm glad I'm not a "cat" person, she thought, and remembered fleetingly the warmth of Paul's deep brown eyes. Eyes of love, she reminded herself, and hurried to catch up.

'Sorry I was late,' he said now, adjusting his stride to match hers. 'I was involved and couldn't get away.'

Torey's lips pursed. Apparently J.B. by any other name was still J.B.! What girl hadn't he been able to leave this time? she wondered. How often in the past had she overheard him say to his roommate, Mick, 'Sorry I'm late but there was this chick . . .' or 'I met a girl in a bar and one thing led to another and . . .' and his blue eyes would glitter with remembered passion, and Torey would lie there on her beach towel silently, her stomach tightening in knots. 'That's quite all right,' she said coolly. 'You needn't have bothered to meet me anyway.'

'Oh, I'd do anything for Addie,' he said quickly, and she thought, There, Torey, serves you right. It's Gran he's trying to please, not you.

'Have you known her long?' Torey asked.

'Five years,' he said. He threaded his way through the hordes of passengers milling at the exit with the same ease as she remembered him cutting through the waves.

'Five years?' she echoed. Was that possible? 'You've lived in the apartment *five* years?' No one lived on The Strand for *five* years! People picked up and moved every three months.

'Mmmm.' His glance was mocking, as though he'd guessed what she was thinking and it amused him. 'Everyone has to live somewhere,' he said lightly.

'Yes, but . . .'

'But what?' He was leading her past rows of cars and she was speculating on which one was his. The blue Corvette? The Porsche? When she had known him he had driven a flashy red MG.

'It—it just surprised me, that's all,' she said, avoiding his eyes. 'Most people don't stay in that part of Manhattan Beach so long.'

'You're right, they don't. It's a nice place to be when you're single though,' he told her, then deftly unlocked the camper door on a brown, late model pick-up truck and tossed her suitcase inside. 'This is it,' he said unnecessarily.

Torey stared. A brown, non-descript pick-up camper? J.B.?

'Not grand enough?' His eyes mocked her again.

'Of course it's grand enough. I drove a Chevvy on the farm. I'm just surprised.' She laughed reflectively. 'I seem to be saying that a lot.'

'You do,' Jake agreed. 'Too many preconceived notions maybe?' He raised a dark eyebrow as he helped her into the truck and then shut the door with a bang, not giving her a chance to reply. What did he mean, preconceived notions, anyway? All her 'notions'—especially about him—were soundly based on fact. And experience. A few surprises weren't going to change that. They just made her more wary, that was all.

She glanced at him surreptitiously, seeing the sun glint off his wristwatch, tracing the chest-hugging T-shirt, and noting the way his jeans moved like a second skin when he depressed the clutch to shift gears. She shook her head, half in amusement, half in wonder. Imagine sitting next to J.B. in a pick-up truck driving down Sepulveda Boulevard! The girl she had been would have swooned at the thought. It was a blessing she was a woman. She looked away, feigning interest in a fancy, new high-rise office tower. It was a blessing she had become Paul Cooper's wife.

'Been here before, have you?' Jake asked, glancing over at her.

'Mmmm. Years ago.'

'Changed much?'

'Yes.' She knew he meant the area, but she couldn't help thinking that that wasn't all that had changed. She wasn't the child she had been then. Was he the same man? In looks at least he wasn't noticeably different—

older, of course, his features more sharply honed, harsher perhaps. Hard living? she wondered. Too much partying, too many women, too many years spent running around? She looked at his hand resting on the window edge, the dark hairs ruffled by the wind. He wore no rings. And he had said that Manhattan was great if you were single. Did that mean he had escaped the 'noose' that he had once, jokingly, called marriage? Most likely. She couldn't imagine who would have been able to settle him down.

'Addie will be glad to see you.'

Torey smiled. 'Yes. It's been several years since she was back in Illinois.'

'You should've come out here.'

'It would have been lovely,' she said wistfully. 'But in the summer we—we were farming, and in the winter, well—the money just wasn't there. We needed all we had just to keep things going.' She didn't know why she was explaining such things to him. J.B. wasn't the sort who had been 'into responsibility' much, as he would have said then. The fancy-free existence he prized wasn't the sort that she had shared with Paul. It was the very thing Jake had scorned about her in fact. 'Anyway,' she said flatly, 'I'm here now.'

'I'm sorry about your husband,' Jake said softly, not looking at her.

Torey looked at him sharply.

'Addie talks about you all a lot,' he went on. 'I moved into her apartment shortly after you and Paul were married.' He grinned slightly. 'You were a lovely bride. I saw all the pictures.'

Torey wanted to sink through the floor. 'You're kidding.'

'No. Not right away of course. Actually not until—until after Paul's accident. It must have been awful for you.'

'It was.' She didn't want to talk about Paul now. Not with Jake. It would be like trying to blend two totally unrelated times in her life. She had never talked about J.B. to Paul. What would there have been to say, really? And she couldn't talk to this man—this stranger— about her husband.

'It isn't much farther now, is it?' she asked. They were turning down a wide, eucalyptus-lined street heading west again, and Torey thought she saw some familiar sights. She hoped so anyway. She needed to get out of this truck. She was tired and she wanted to see her grandmother. But mostly she wanted to get rid of Jake Brosnan.

'Almost there. Pier's right over the next hill.'

Manhattan Beach had changed and yet it hadn't over the past seven years. Many buildings were new, but trendy boutiques and beach apparel shops still proliferated; different girls wore the same miniscule Hawaiian print bikinis; and sand-encrusted young men with zinc oxide-coated noses carried the same surfboards down the hills. The same, but different. Like Jake Brosnan, perhaps?

'Tired?' Jake asked.

'Definitely.'

'You have a rest then, and later I'll take you to visit Addie.'

Torey stared. 'What? Visit Addie where?'

'The nursing home,' Jake said as if she was the one confused. And she was.

'She's not home?'

'Not 'til you get there,' Jake said. 'Doctors orders. I volunteered to keep an eye on her, but it wasn't good enough. They had to have you.' He grinned. 'I hope you're worth your fancy degree.'

Torey looked at him, baffled.

'You do have a degree in physiotherapy?'

'Yes, but . . .'

'Well, that's what they're waiting for. None of the rest of us mortals are any good apparently. At least I wasn't. And no other physiotherapist was good enough for Addie but you. She told the doctor that.' He grinned, obviously remembering a scene between her feisty grandmother and the doctor. 'Anyhow, now that you're here, she gets to come home tomorrow.' He zipped down an alley and swung the truck into a garage. 'Come on,' he said, hopping out and fetching her suitcase, leaving Torey to follow him through the gate and into the tiny, bricked-over back yard she remembered so well. Some of the same rusty, old toy trucks were in the sand box. Along with a new Fisher-Price steam roller and dump truck. Trust Gran to continue to provide toys for the neighbourhood, Torey thought. Jake stepped over a frisbee and unlocked the back door.

'You remember Maynard, don't you?' he asked her, and she saw the old Irish Setter lying under the table, thumping his tail for all he was worth.

'Of course.' Torey felt a wave of nostalgia wash over her as she bent to scratch Maynard's ears. How many times had she sat on those very same back steps and mooned over J.B., her face pressed against the red of Maynard's glossy coat? She stood up again to see that Jake had disappeared with her suitcase.

'I put it in the back bedroom,' he told her, wiping his hands on the seat of his jeans and then glancing at his watch.

'Can I—can I offer you a glass of ice water?' Torey fumbled, feeling totally inadequate as a hostess. He knew his way around her grandmother's house better than she did!

'Thanks, no,' he said. 'I've got to run. Get some rest now. I stocked the refrigerator and cupboards if you get hungry. I'll pick you up about three-thirty, okay?'

'Sure, that's fine,' she said, wishing she could find some reason to object. A whole day of Jake Brosnan was not exactly what she had in mind. 'If Gran's car works, I could drive myself,' she said lamely.

'Sure,' Jake scoffed good-naturedly. 'And Addie'd

have my head on a plate. No thanks. Scott and I will pick you up.'

Torey smiled at that. At least they wouldn't be alone. She was glad that Gran had such nice young neighbours that they would take the time to visit her. 'Who's Scott?' she asked as Jake went down the back steps.

He looked back over his shoulder, the sun catching the angles of his face. 'My son,' he said. 'Scott's my son.'

CHAPTER TWO

'YOUR son?' she echoed, but he had already turned and was striding across the yard with the easy, graceful movements she had carried in her mind's eye for the past seven years. He pounded up the stairs to his apartment over the garage, and she heard a faint off-key whistling before the door shut behind him.

So Jake Brosnan had a son. A miniature of himself no doubt. He would have made a devilish child—the grooved cheeks mere dimples in a boy, the straight teeth now, once a gap-toothed grin. Jake as a child—it didn't bear thinking about. She shut Gran's kitchen door and began poking through the cupboards to find herself a snack. Jake was right, the cupboards were well-stocked. Peanut butter, jam, canned goods, freshly baked whole-wheat bread, apparently brought from the bakery. Jake had certainly been thorough. Damn. She didn't want to think about him. She made herself a sandwich and poured a glass of milk, taking both out into the living room where she could sit in Gran's rocking chair and look out the bay window across the minute front yard and down to the broad sidewalk called The Strand which bordered on the vast expanse of sandy beach.

The room was almost exactly as she had remembered it, with heavy oak and mahogany furniture so far out of style to be coming back in with the young set, and a faded braid rug on the polished, hardwood floor. A sea of family pictures flooded every available surface. Small wonder Jake had seen her wedding pictures if he had been in this room! Gran might be a long way from the family, but they were never out of sight nor, apparently, out of mind.

Setting her glass down, Torey crossed the room and

22

took her wedding picture off Gran's television set. She couldn't even feel really sad looking at it despite knowing how things had turned out. It had been such a happy day, so bright, so sunny, so full of promise. Paul was grinning as though he had just pulled off the biggest coup of the century, and she—Torey looked at her younger self, at the girl with the long black hair and sparkling green eyes smiling up at her new husband— she looked as though she had come home at last.

Sighing, Torey set the picture back on to the TV. Maybe we were too happy, she thought, not for the first time. Maybe it wasn't meant to last. But, she reminded herself roughly, thinking that way was foolish. Marrying Paul for however long it lasted was the best thing that had ever happened to her. It had shown her what true love was all about, and it reinforced her notions about the shallowness of men like Jake Brosnan. Thank God her infatuation with him had been just that.

Maynard ambled out and lay his head in her lap as she sat and rocked in the chair. She patted his head, loving the silky feel of his ears, and said, 'Remember me, old pal?'

Maynard's tail thumped enthusiastically.

Torey hugged him. 'Good. You do. My favourite confidant—and most discreet one, too. You never repeated a thing I told you.' She ruffled his fur. 'Stand by, Maynard,' she whispered into his ear. 'You got me through Jake Brosnan once. You might have to do it again.' It wasn't something she wanted to think about, but it was there. The attraction, that is. Shallow and insubstantial though it might be, even after seven years she still felt it. Damn, again.

Maynard's tail waved like a flag in a stiff wind when he heard her say 'Jake' and Torey wrinkled her nose at him. 'He's your friend, I suppose,' she said gruffly. 'Gone over to the enemy, have you?'

Maynard whined and flipped her hand back on to his head with his long nose, as if demanding that she keep stroking him. Torey shook her head. 'Sorry, pup, nap-time. Got to be on my toes for Gran.' And for Jake Brosnan, she thought wryly, dumping her empty plate into the sink and going into the tiny back bedroom where she had slept that summer long ago. She drew back the chenille spread and undressed down to her slip, stretching out under the thin blanket and staring at the sprigs of lavender on the pale wallpaper by her head. She wanted to sleep or to remember Paul or, at the very least, to run through in her head the sort of physical therapy that she should begin with Gran. But she couldn't think of a thing—but Jake. And his son. And, she mused, presumably a wife. Who had Jake married? Anyone she had known? He'd had no steady girl in those days. If ever a man could have been said to 'play the field', it was Jake. What sort of a husband had he become? Not one like Paul, she was certain. Was he even still married? He'd mentioned his son, but not his wife. But then, she'd hardly evinced any interest. And he'd never struck her as the type who would be saying first off, 'You'll have to meet my wife.' The Jake she had known could just as easily have forgotten he had one. It was not difficult to assume that he hadn't really changed. We'll see, she thought. We'll see this son and this wife. And she closed her eyes, consumed by curiosity and, perhaps, a touch of something else.

'She's still sleeping!' The childish voice bellowed inches from her ear, and Torey snapped upright, blinking and disoriented. Solemn blue eyes beneath a fringe of flaxen hair regarded her curiously. 'She's not sleepin' now, Dad,' the boy yelled, never blinking once.

Torey's brows drew together in a frown. *This* was Scott? Of course there was no question about it. Why else would he be standing at her bedside announcing her sleeping habits to his invisible father? But a miniature Jake he was not. Obviously he took after his mother. His hair, already blond, was bleached almost

white by the sun, and his nose, she imagined, must wear
a perpetual sunburn while his father only tanned. At
least, she thought, Scott had blue eyes, though they
were the warm blue of a Caribbean lagoon, not the
arctic blue of Jake's. He was clearly older than her
three-year-old niece, Tracy, and when he opened his
mouth to speak she saw a bottom tooth missing. At
least she had guessed something right.

'You must be Scott,' she said, brushing stray tendrils
of hair out of her eyes.

'Yep. Come on, get up so's we can go see Addie.' He
looked at her beseechingly.

Torey swung her legs off the bed and stood up.
'Okay. Scoot on out of here now and tell your father I'll
be ready in a few minutes.'

'She'll be ready in a few minutes,' Scott hollered, not
budging from her side.

'Not with your help, fella,' Jake said, materialising in
the doorway and regarding Torey's dishevelment and
state of undress with a lazy grin. 'Sorry if he woke you,'
he told her, but he was grinning as if he had engineered
the whole thing. Torey gave him a sour look.

'We'll just wait in the living room,' Jake said, but his
eyes were undressing her faster than she could pull
herself together.

'Do that,' Torey said in a clipped tone, and moved
towards him, herding Scott in front of her, shutting the
door on their backs with a loud click. Damn him,
anyway. She could feel her cheeks burning as she
remembered his expression, and she made a face at the
closed door before she hurriedly opened her suitcase,
rooting through it for a hair brush and some clean
white jeans and a blue chambray shirt, made for Paul,
which she hastily donned. She knotted the tails on the
shirt leaving a discreet amount of tanned midriff visible.
Let him look at that, she thought angrily. No doubt he
would. The interest he had shown in her with that look
made Vince Liebfried and Harlan Nelson seem blind by

comparison. She snorted and banged the suitcase shut.
So much for escaping the masculine eye!

It would take too long to re-plait her hair neatly, so
she pulled it back at the nape of her neck and tied a
navy silk scarf around it, leaving the thick wavy tresses
to cascade loosely down her back. It was no wonder he
hadn't recognised her. Seven years ago her hair hadn't
been any longer than Scott's—a feathery, pixie cut that
she had begun to grow out as soon as she had returned
home. She applied a coating of coral lip gloss and
regarded herself solemnly for a moment. Then she took
a deep breath and went out to face Jake Brosnan and
his most surprising son.

Jake was standing with his back to her, staring out
the window at the beach when she entered the living
room. It was Scott, who had been idly plunking out
Peter, Peter, Pumpkin Eater on the piano, who said,
'Super, you're ready. C'mon, Dad. Let's go.' He
bounced off the piano bench and hurtled out the door,
letting the screen bang shut behind him.

'A ball of energy, isn't he?' Torey said, watching him
depart.

Jake's mouth quirked in a grin. 'And how.'

'He must be about five?' Torey speculated as she
followed Scott down the steps while Jake locked the
door.

'He'll be six in August,' Jake replied. 'On Addie's
birthday.'

Torey smiled. 'She must love that—sharing a
birthday.' It was exactly the sort of thing that would
appeal to her grandmother.

Jake nodded. 'They both do. It's a mutual admiration
society.' He shook his head. 'She's an incredible old
lady. Sometimes I don't know what I'd do without her,'
he added almost to himself.

Torey looked at him curiously, having a surprising
amount of difficulty thinking of Jake Brosnan as a
father. It didn't fit with what she thought she

remembered of him. But there was no doubt about it—the blond dynamo in the car was calling, 'Hurry up, Dad! C'mon! Addie'll have a cow if we aren't there soon.'

'A cow, is it?' Jake grinned. 'A lady the size of Addie? A kitten more likely, sport,' he said to his son. 'Shove over so Victoria can get in.'

'Torey,' Torey corrected. 'Only Gran ever calls me Victoria.'

'Torey then.' Jake seemed to savour the name on his lips, and gave her a smile that would have melted her seven years ago. It caused her knees to quake even now.

'Can I sit by the window?' Scott asked, looking from his father to Torey.

Jake shrugged. 'It's up to Torey.'

Thanks, Torey thought drily. Just what she wanted—even greater proximity to Jake Brosnan. But how could you say no to a face like Scott's? 'Sure,' she said, and was rewarded by a toothless grin.

'Addie's sure gonna be glad to see you,' Scott told her as they got underway. 'She's been wantin' to come home forever. When she comes home we're gonna play trucks, and I'm gonna play her piano instead of her havin' to play for me, and I'll play her lots of games of Snap before I go to school. D'you play Snap?' He cocked his head with sudden interest, as though sizing up a potential partner.

'I am a whiz,' Torey told him. 'It sounds like you and Addie have a grand time.' It sounded like they were together every waking moment. Where was Jake? And his wife?

'We do,' Scott replied. 'We played together every morning 'til she had her operation.'

'Every morning?' Torey probed. How convenient for Jake—a built-in babysitter. It figured. Still no sense of responsibility. She edged slightly away from the taut blue jean clad thigh only centimetres from her own.

'Yeah, I miss her,' Scott let out a long, agonised sigh,

and Torey found herself wanting to giggle. 'It's good you're here 'cause you can teach her to walk with her new knee. Dad said nobody else knew how. You must be pretty smart,' Scott reflected. 'Besides bein' pretty,' he added. 'My dad thinks you're . . .'

'Show Torey where you go to school,' Jake interrupted, and Scott's attention veered as he pointed out the low tan buildings they were just passing on the left.

Your dad thinks what? Torey wondered, but she wondered in vain for the next thing Scott said was, 'Addie said you had a farm. Can you milk a cow?' and her descriptions of the farm that she and Paul had been buying kept them going conversationally until Jake pulled into the parking lot outside a Spanish style building with a splash of burgundy coloured bougainvillaea climbing the walls and said, 'Here we are. Calling in all bets. Is your money on the kitten or the cow?'

Torey laughed. 'How about just a monumental fit of impatience? That ought to just about sum it up if I know Gran.'

'About time,' Addie Harrison said, her normally steady voice wavering slightly as she looked her beloved granddaughter up and down. 'Don't just stand there. A hug hasn't broken me yet.' And Torey, tears shimmering, flew into her grandmother's arms, sinking to her knees before the wheelchair and laying her head against Gran's breast. For the moment Jake Brosnan totally disappeared. There was only Addie in the room—Addie who had sized Paul up the day of the wedding and nodded her head. 'You'll do, young man,' she had said. 'I couldn't have picked a finer one than you.' Torey felt her grandmother's arms tighten around her, a hug of welcome, a hug of comfort. She knew Addie, too, was remembering her last visit to Galena when Torey and Paul had been married just a year. 'You're a lucky woman,' she had told her granddaughter then. 'He's a keeper, just like your grandad was. Seeing marriages fall apart right and left, I'm just so glad all's well with you.' Torey sniffed and dabbed ineffectually at her eyes, pulling back slightly and looking up into the dear, familiar eyes, suddenly aware of other people in the room. Gran's eyes smiled into hers a second longer before lifting to share her joy with other eyes. Jake's.

Torey struggled to her feet, feeling awkward, wishing the eyes watching her were anyone's other than his. But when she glanced at him she saw neither the indulgent amusement or mocking grin that she anticipated, but a look of tenderness that unnerved her. Hurriedly she looked around for Scott.

He reappeared with a glass of lemonade in his hand. 'You done cryin' now?' he asked. 'Dad said to scram while you . . .'

'Dad should have said to keep your mouth shut too,' Jake said gruffly, rapping his knuckles softly on the boy's fair hair.

'Nonsense,' Addie said. 'Out of the mouths of babes and all that.'

'Exactly what I'm afraid of,' Jake retorted, grinning.

'Has Jake helped you get settled in?' Gran asked Torey.

'Oh, uh, yes. I really don't need much help,' Torey said quickly.

'I'm sure Jake must be very busy'—with whatever he was "involved in" now, she thought—'and I can easily manage without him.'

'Well, I can't,' her grandmother said flatly. 'I don't know what I would do without Jake.'

Torey groaned inwardly. All she needed was to hear what a paragon Jake Brosnan was.

'He shops for me, he weeds for me, he walks Maynard for me,' Gran catalogued. 'He can fix plumbing and change fuses and. . .'

'And I'm housebroken, too,' Jake said with an almost sheepish grin. 'She's president of my fan club,' he explained, winking at Gran.

'With a membership in the thousands, I'm sure,' Torey said more sharply than she intended. After all he probably didn't put the make on little old ladies. Gran's infatuation with him, at least, could be excused.

'Oh, at least,' he answered airily. 'Want to sign up?'

'I'm afraid I'm a bit more choosy than that.'

'Victoria!' Addie exclaimed, shocked, and Torey felt her cheeks redden. Why couldn't she just be polite and indifferent to him? Why did she have to leap at his baited hooks like some dumb fish? It was as though nothing had changed from seven years ago. Could she never stop acting like a besotted adolescent around him?

'Excuse me,' she apologised demurely. 'I didn't mean to be rude.' She cast a desperate glance towards the door, not completely disguising her wish to bolt through it and get away from him, when she heard Jake say to her grandmother, 'My fault, really, Addie. I shouldn't tease.'

Just what she needed, him taking the blame for her own rudeness. Damn the man! Torey shoved her hair back over her shoulder and said with forced lightness, 'Scott says that you two play together in the mornings.'

'Every day,' Gran agreed. 'He keeps me on my toes.' She ruffled the small boy's hair. 'We have a good time, don't we?' she said to Scott.

'Super,' Scott agreed. 'And can she cook! Did she make you those good raisin cookies when you were little?' he asked Torey.

'Definitely,' Torey told him. 'Even mailed them to us after we were married . . .' Her voice drifted off, oddly reluctant to talk about her marriage to Paul in front of Jake. He seemed to watch her so intently. When Scott had asked about milking the cows, in the car, and she had been explaining about their farm, Jake's whole body had tensed rather like Maynard when he spotted an intruder. She sensed the same thing now, a tautness and an intensity that unnerved her.

'We'll make some more when I get home,' Addie promised. 'And Torey can help. Would you like that?'

'What about Dad, can't he?'

'I have to work,' Jake said, and Torey wondered what he was doing these days. Seven years ago he had been a graphic artist for a large advertising firm. She remembered once plucking up enough courage to ask him a direct question, was he a flight test engineer like Mick? And he had laughed. 'Hardly,' he had said. 'I draw breath mints.' She had stared, astonished, and he had laughed again with a scorn that she didn't think was entirely directed at her, and then he shrugged, explaining, 'I draw ads. I'm an artist—of a sort.' And apparently he didn't think much of the sort of artist he was. Finding out, though, had shed some light on one of his more curious habits. Very often that summer she had seen him on the beach with a sketchpad in his hand. Sometimes he would be down early, close to the shore watching the birds darting through the tide; at other times she would see him watching a volleyball game, making quick rapid strokes on a pad of paper; and now and then she found him on the crest of sand above the high tide mark where he could see the line of surfers far out, a hand shading his eyes as he glanced from the tiny figures on their boards to the sketches he was making. Those were the times, she knew, when drawing breath mints was the farthest thing from his mind. Was he still drawing them? she wondered.

'Jake is an illustrator,' Addie explained. 'Children's books, mostly.' She motioned to Scott to fetch one off her bedside table. 'I sent Debbie's little girl his latest last Christmas.' And Scott handed Torey a copy of Tracy's favourite, most dog-eared book, one that Auntie Torey had read to her several thousand times.

'You're *that* James Brosnan?' she asked, astonished.

Jake's cheekbones flushed, and he cleared his throat

with a nervousness that almost made her smile. He seemed nearly as uncomfortable acknowledging this as he had the breath mints! 'Yeah.'

'Your books are wonderful,' Torey told him, and there could be no doubting the sincerity in her voice. The one she was holding was an Irish folk tale retold by an excellent children's author and illustrated in droll water colours and pen-and-ink drawings with just enough caricature to muse without the distortion that would mask the humanity of the characters. It was a very long way from breath mints, and Torey could scarcely believe that the Jake Brosnan she had known was the man who had drawn them.

'Thanks.' He ducked his dark head in the way of a small boy receiving an unaccustomed compliment, and when he lifted it he was grinning. 'Change your mind about the fan club?' he asked irrepressibly.

Torey laughed. 'I'll think about it.'

'That's promising,' Gran said. 'I think you should press your advantage, Jake. Take her to dinner.'

'What? But, Gran, I . . .' Torey began.

'Great idea,' Jake said. 'D'you like pizza?'

'Yes, but . . .'

'Oh boy, pizza!' Scott exclaimed.

'You don't need to . . .'

'Of course he doesn't need to. He *wants* to,' Addie said authoritatively.

'But . . .' But Torey could see that she was getting nowhere at all. They were all three grinning at her, and Scott was bouncing up and down saying, 'Please, please, please,' as though it was a mantra, and so she shrugged and said, 'Why not?' thinking that perhaps Debbie had been right after all. Maybe she had played right into her mother's hands. There was one thing certain—resisting Jake Brosnan was going to be a much greater challenge than ignoring Vince Liebfried and Harlan Nelson. But if she didn't she was, indeed, a fool. The last thing she needed in her life after a wonderful man like Paul was a shallow, bedhopping heartbreaker like Jake Brosnan!

'We'll be by to get you in the early afternoon,' Jake promised Addie, and bent down to give her a kiss.

Torey felt it as if he had given it to her. The warm, hard lips had seared her flesh, branding her for all time, on a hot mid-August night seven years ago, and she had repressed it all not long after. But now the memory flooded back. The feelings, the emotions, the desire all poured into her mind, and she gripped the end of Gran's bed, her knuckles whitening with the strain of not reaching out for him.

'Torey?' Gran looked at her with concern. 'Are you all right?'

'Hmm? Oh, oh yes, fine,' Torey mumbled, sucking in a long draught of air. 'Just a bit of jet lag, I expect.'

'Very likely,' her grandmother agreed, but she still regarded her granddaughter curiously. 'Don't keep her up 'till all hours, Jake,' she warned, eyes twinkling.

'No,' he agreed. 'We'll go to bed early.' He shot Torey a teasing grin that dared her to comment on his outrageous statement, and she opened and closed her mouth like a fish before she managed to splutter one.

'Say goodbye to Addie, Scott. We've got to feed your father soon. He's obviously getting light-headed.'

'Light-headed, am I?' Jake grinned as he herded Torey and Scott towards the truck. 'Why? Because I want to go to bed with you?'

'Jake!'

'Well?' He was gazing at her unrepentantly, and she thought, how like the Jake of old that was. In those days he had made no bones about lusting after first one and then another of the bikini clad girls who swished up and down the beach. But then, at least, he had been free to do so. Now he seemed to have conveniently misplaced his wife!

'*I* don't want to go to bed with *you*!' she hissed, grateful that Scott had run ahead. 'Just because I'm a widow doesn't mean that I am automatically in the market for a man'

'Did I say you were?' He held the door for her, shutting it after Scott clambered up beside her, and she thought how ironic it was that they could be having an argument about her going to bed with him while he was acting a perfect gentleman and they were going out for pizza with his son!

'I don't want to talk about it,' she snapped when he opened the driver's side door and swung into the cab beside her.

'Not now, perhaps,' he agreed, his gaze resting momentarily on Scott. 'But don't consider the subject dropped.'

'It *is* dropped.'

'Then I'll just have to pick it up again,' he said, his blue eyes unsettling as they raked over her, 'at a more convenient time.'

The truce, if you could call it that, lasted until the waitress took their order and Jake gave Scott a fistful of pennies to ride the mechanical horse that was provided for the amusement of the younger diners. Then Jake stretched out lazily in the chair across from Torey, his loafer clad foot grazing her ankle under the table. 'Now then, about our discussion,' he began, sipping from his glass of beer and making Torey feel like a rabbit trapped by a very hungry wolf.

'We have nothing to discuss,' Torey said, thanking God that he had never looked at her like this seven years ago. If he had, the silly girl she had been would have fallen at his feet.

'Scared?' he teased.

'No.' Annoyed was more like it. Who did he think he was? And didn't his wife care, for God's sake, if he went around propositioning every girl he met? Well, Torey admitted, perhaps she didn't. There were women like that around, women who wanted their freedom too. And maybe Jake had found himself one of them. 'Just wondering,' she said sweetly, 'how your wife fits into this little seduction scheme?'

Jake jerked upright. 'My wife?'

'Well, perhaps you don't have to have a wife to have a son,' Torey went on, 'but I should think it would be easier that way.'

Jake took a long swallow of beer. 'It was,' he said flatly. 'I don't have a wife now. We're divorced.' He glared at Torey as though it were somehow her fault. 'You thought I was coming on to you like that while I had a wife tucked away somewhere?' he demanded.

Torey shrugged, feeling defensive and not knowing why. 'It seemed likely,' she said stonily.

'Why?' His voice was as icy as his eyes.

'Sleeping around just seemed your style,' she said indifferently, swirling the beer in her glass, staring at the golden liquid and avoiding his frosty gaze.

'What the hell do you know about my style?' he bit out.

'You'd be amazed.' He would, too.

'What'd Addie say to you, for God's sake? I never . . .'

'Not Gran,' Torey said. 'Gran thinks you're God's gift to women apparently. Who am I to disillusion her?'

'Who else then?' Jake was completely disconcerted now. He eyed her narrowly, and she wished the pizza would come before he took a bite out of her.

'Let's just say, I've had a bit of experience too.'

'It's not my fault you met some bastard in your past,' Jake said.

'It is if the bastard was you.'

'What?' He choked on his beer.

'Oh, it wasn't entirely your fault,' Torey said. 'I was a silly, naïve child, I admit it. Actually I suppose I should thank you for it. I mean, I went home and began going out with Paul again and . . .'

'What in bloody hell are you talking about?'

Torey looked over at him, seeing confusion in the

hooded eyes. 'You really don't remember, do you?' she sighed. 'Well, I guess my name was legion that summer.' And probably plenty of summers since, she thought cynically.

'What summer? When?'

The waitress slapped a pizza down between them and Torey looked around to call Scott, but Jake shook his head. 'Don't. He likes it cold just as well, and he's bound to have a few pennies left. What summer are you talking about?' He reached across the table to grip her wrist in his hand. 'Tell me.'

'Seven years ago. I was out here spending the summer with my grandparents. You were living in an apartment on The Strand with a guy named Mick . . .' Her voice trailed off at the tightening in Jake's features.

'Go on,' he said tersely.

Torey shrugged helplessly. 'I had a crush on you. Typical teenage stuff. I wasn't very sophisticated, and you were.'

Jake's mouth twisted. He was staring hard at her, as though trying to remember her from another age.

'All summer long I trailed around after you. Worshipping from afar mostly.' Torey managed a shaky laugh, wishing that she'd never started this. Whatever had made her think that it would be easier to deal with him if he knew? She took a gulp of beer in hope that it would steady her. 'Your friend Mick was very perceptive. He knew how I felt, and once he invited me along on a double date. Him and a stewardess named Cathy or something . . .'

'Christy,' Jake supplied abruptly. He shut his eyes and bent his dark head. 'I remember,' he said slowly. For a long moment neither of them said a word. The clatter of pinball and the whirring noises of the video games stretched between them like an ocean. 'Mick must've been out of his mind,' he said finally, shaking his head.

'He thought he was doing me a favour,' Torey said. 'He didn't realise that I wasn't exactly in your league.'

Jake shook his head wryly. 'God, what a mess.' He cut a piece of pizza and handed it to her on a plate. Torey took it and concentrated on the pizza, remembering that awful night with a clarity she hadn't achieved in years, and one glance at Jake's face told her that he had his memories too.

Mick had recruited her at the last moment to go to a concert when Jake's current date couldn't come. 'We've already got the tickets. Hey, really, J.B. won't mind,' he had said, giving her an encouraging grin. He knew she was crazy about J.B.—he was a quieter, more observant type than his roommate when it came to other people. There was no doubt he could have a 'good time' as much as any of the other swinging bachelors who lived near the beach, but she had never seen him pursue his amusements as frenetically as J.B. seemed to. And she was far enough gone over J.B. to believe him. If he thought she could keep J.B. interested for an evening, who was she to say no?

So she had gone, shaking with trepidation at the thought of actually being J.B.'s date. And well she might have, for if the concert went all right, the party afterwards was a disaster. The four of them went back to somebody's apartment—Torey never even knew whose, and she wasn't sure that J.B. knew either— where the lights were dim, the atmosphere smoky with things besides tobacco, and the music loud enough to raise the dead. J.B. had looked at her sourly when she asked only for a Coke, but he got it for her, taking something far stronger himself. Torey watched him drink it, wishing she could think of something scintillating to say, something that *Seventeen* magazine guaranteed would make him ask her out again—but nothing came to mind. The Coke was warm and flat, the music deafening, and the crush of people soon had J.B.'s hot, perspiration-soaked body pressed against hers. 'Let's get outa here,' he muttered in her ear, slipping an arm around her waist and ushering her towards the door, jostling other straining, gyrating bodies as they went.

'But what about Mick . . .' she began, but J.B. just shook his head.

'Who needs Mick?' and he had opened the door and they were alone. At first Torey had been relieved. The music receded, the hot bodies vanished, she was alone with J.B.—just like in one of her millions of summertime fantasies. And then the panic began to set in.

They walked the few yards across The Strand down to the beach, Torey's hand engulfed in J.B.'s warm one, and then, without warning, he pulled her down on the sand, his arms going around her tightly, caressing up and down her spine, his breath hot and rum-scented on her face. 'Oh God, love, let me . . .' he muttered, his lips pressed against her throat.

Torey stiffened, struggled, revelling in his passion at the same moment that it frightened her out of her wits! J.B.'s hands were busy unfastening her blouse, moving against the smooth flesh of her stomach, sliding under her bra to mould her breasts, and Torey reached up wildly trying to drag his hands away. This wasn't what she had fantasised at all.

'Please,' she muttered. 'Oh, please . . .' Polite to the last, she thought now, with a wry humour that had definitely escaped her at the time. But J.B. hadn't responded to politeness, or if he had, it was because he thought she'd meant 'please continue', not 'please stop'. Finally, desperate, she had kicked him in the shin, wrenching away from him, and rolled sobbing on the sand.

'Christ,' he muttered, rubbing his leg. 'You're a damned wildcat, you know that?' He was looking at her like he'd never seen such behaviour before. Even in the dimness of the streetlight she could see his puzzlement. 'Mick said you liked me,' he went on. 'You got a damn funny way of showing it.'

'Liking you and doing ... doing ... that ...' Torey gulped, rubbing a sandy hand across her face, 'are two different things.'

J.B. snorted. 'Not in my book, babe. You been coming on to me all night.'

'I have not!'

He rubbed a weary hand against the back of his neck. 'Oh Jesus, you probably don't even know what you're doing. How the hell old are you anyway?'

'Eighteen,' she admitted, not looking at him, burning enough as it was under the glare of his gaze.

J.B. groaned and said a rude word, reaching out and hauling her unceremoniously to her feet. 'Figures,' he said. 'Damn Mick anyway. He said you were nice.'

'I *am* nice,' Torey retorted, resenting the way he was dragging her across the sand, stumbling as her shoes came off.

'Not the way he means,' J.B. said flatly. 'Or the way I thought he meant,' he amended.

'Where are you taking me?' she demanded as he tugged her along The Strand completely oblivious to the stares of passersby.

'Home. Where else?'

'But ...' She couldn't go home now. Not looking like this, dishevelled, tear-streaked, covered with sand. 'My grandmother ...'

J.B. groaned again. 'Geez, a grandmother no less.' He sounded thoroughly disgusted. His eyes flew heavenward, and Torey wished she'd kept her mouth shut. But then he sighed and said, 'All right. Come to my place and clean up. But then it's home for you, understand?'

Torey understood. He took her back to his apartment, looking to the right and left as though he were expecting either an irate grandmother or the entire local police force to spring out at him as he unlocked the door. Once they were inside he pointed her in the direction of the bathroom, saying, 'Ten minutes. Snap to it.' It wasn't the way her fantasies had envisioned her arrival in J.B.'s apartment at all. In them he had carried her over the threshold, looking down at her with passion-filled, adoring eyes, and had taken her into his bedroom where slowly and leisurely, with infinite gentleness, he had made her a woman.

Instead she was staring into his cracked bathroom mirror, trying to wash the streaky tears off her face and blot the puffiness away from her eyes, all the while wondering if those were his blue trunks hanging over the showerhead, and if it was he or Mick who had left the cap off the toothpaste beside the sink. Moments later the banging on the door caused her to jump.

'Finished?' J.B. demanded.

'Almost.' Her voice was still shaky. She ran her fingers through her short, fluffy hair-do, trying to make it look windblown not attacked.

'Hurry up.'

She didn't hear him move away, and she took a moment longer to rearrange her gauzy peasant blouse and tuck it back into her skirt with trembling fingers before she opened the door to face him. He was leaning against the wall opposite, staring at her from beneath hooded eyelids. His face was tight, grim, about as unloving as one could imagine. So much for fantasies.

He took her by the arm and escorted her to the door as though he could hardly wait to get her out of his apartment. 'You're not from around here, are you?' he asked as they began to walk the two blocks to her grandparents' home.

'No.'

'Take my advice,' he said, his voice rough and hard. 'Go home and grow up before you try a trick like this again.'

'What trick?'

'Playing grown-up. You don't belong here.'

'And you do?' she demanded, close to tears again.

'I know what I'm doing,' he said gruffly. 'You don't.'

They had reached her grandparents' house now, and she could see in through the bay window. Her grandfather was reading the evening paper and her grandmother was watching television. Homey. Comfortable. J.B. looked through the window too, considering the scene inside.

'It figures,' he muttered. 'Go on in.'

Torey looked at him hesitantly, her eyes flickering over his rigid shoulders and the angry features shadowed beneath the dark hair. 'Good night,' she murmured and went up the front steps, pausing as she turned the doorknob. 'Thank you.'

'Thank you?' J.B. sounded incredulous. 'Jesus.' And he turned and was striding down the walk towards The Strand before she even got inside.

'The pizza's cold,' Scott complained as he slipped into the chair beside her. 'Why didn't you call me?'

Jake shrugged, apparently as incapable as Torey of saying anything at the moment. His pizza lay equally cold and uneaten on his plate. He tipped the last of his beer down his throat and motioned for the waitress to bring a box. 'Come on,' he said brusquely. 'As long as it's cold anyway, we might as well eat it at home.'

Torey got to her feet without a word. She was as unwilling as Jake to go on pretending that they were just another happy family out for a meal. Scott started to whine until Jake fixed him with a glare. That was enough, and Scott, too, lapsed into silence until they reached home.

CHAPTER THREE

'WE need to talk,' Jake said, grabbing Torey's arm to stop her crossing the garden to Addie's house.

'Why?'

Jake looked taken aback. 'Because we . . . you . . .'

'Just because I was once a fool doesn't mean I'm fool enough to want to rehash the past now,' Torey said, tugging her arm out of his.

'No one said you were a fool. Now or then.'

'Perhaps foolishness is in the mind of the beholder then,' Torey said. 'But if you're charitable enough to forget that, be charitable enough to drop the subject, please.'

'C'mon, Dad, let's have the pizza,' Scott implored, grabbing Jake's shirt-tail and tugging him up the stairs.

'Don't you want some?' Jake said to Torey's back, apparently aware that he wouldn't get her up the stairs any other way.

'No thanks, I'm not hungry,' she said without turning around. 'It's been a long day. Good night.'

'We'll talk later then,' he said in the same imperious tone that he had used earlier when he wanted her to know that whatever the subject, it wasn't going to be dropped.

Like hell we will, she thought and went swiftly up Addie's back steps and shut the door firmly behind her. Locked it, too, for she didn't think that barging in was beyond what Jake was capable of. Maynard lifted his head, eyeing her suspiciously. Then, apparently deciding that she posed no real threat to his nap, he thumped his tail a few times and dozed off again.

'Oh Maynard,' Torey groaned, sinking down to the floor to pat his sleek fur. 'I've done it now.' How could she have been so foolish as to bring up the past? He already had enough ideas about her—wanting to go to bed with her, indeed!—and now he was going to think she was just as besotted with him as she had been so many years ago.

Dumb move, Cooper, she chastised herself. It was obvious that Addie was matchmaking—no doubt certain that St James Brosnan was the ideal man with whom to tempt her beloved granddaughter into marriage a second time—and it was equally apparent that, if Jake didn't have marriage in mind, at least he wasn't averse to going to bed with her! Good God, he'd even said so. Some things never change, she told herself. And apparently Jake Brosnan was one of them.

She gave Maynard one last pat and hauled herself to her feet. A hot bath sounded marvellous, therapeutic, just what she needed to help her absorb the shocks of the day. Jake Brosnan, for God's sake! Damn it, she couldn't get him out of her mind. Somewhere in the back of her consciousness she had toyed with the idea of trying to seek him out when she came out to California this time—a possibility somewhat akin to finding a needle in a haystack, she had thought at the time. But it would have been interesting, she thought, to take a look at the man she had considered to be the epitome of manhood when she was a foolish innocent of eighteen. She could have had a good laugh.

So why wasn't she laughing?

You can't seriously still be interested in him, she lectured herself as she lolled neck deep in the lilac scented bubbles. Of course I'm not, she decided firmly, I'm just surprised to see him that's all. He threw me off balance a bit. But since he's here ... since he's here I can prove to myself once and for all that what I felt was just a silly, schoolgirl crush on a wholly inappropriate man. Pity, she thought wryly, he was such a damned attractive inappropriate man. Still, there was more to a man than his looks. She was certainly grown up enough to realise that.

Satisfied, she wrung out the washcloth and lay back in the tub, closing her eyes and drifting on sheer physical sensations—enjoying the languor of her limbs, the gentle lapping of the water against her breasts, the nose-tickling scent of the bubbles caught in the escaping tendrils of her hair.

Then the pounding began. She sprang up, flipping her plait in annoyance with a bubble-covered hand. Damn him anyway! Couldn't he ever take no for an answer? Well, if that was the way he wanted it, so be it. No time like the present for straightening out any misconceptions he might have about how much sweet little Torey was still in love with him!

She yanked the plug out with her toes, shivering in the cool air until she could wrap the huge lavender bath towel around her. Flinging open the door she yelled. 'Hang on a minute, you idiot!' and slammed the door again, briskly rubbing down her slim torso, all languor gone now, replaced by a curiously combative vitality that made her want to flay Jake Brosnan alive.

She slipped into a thin, yellow cotton nightgown and cinched a voluminous terry robe of darker lemon yellow around her and strode out to the kitchen. The pounding had stopped, but Maynard had taken up the banner and was whining at the door with more energy than Torey had seen in him yet.

Torey glared at him. 'The idea, you stupid hound,' she growled, 'is for you to protect me from what is out there, not stand here begging me to let it in.'

Maynard waved his tail enthusiastically, nudging her towards the door. She could see Jake nonchalantly leaning against the porch railing looking for all the world like he was waiting for a bus.

Torey flung open the door and bowed ungraciously. 'Come in if you must,' she said as he brushed past her into the kitchen. All her hearty resolve about putting him in his place suffered an immediate setback. Telling off Jake Brosnan in the abstract was a much easier proposition than facing the living, breathing, virile man in front of her. She took a deep breath and faced him with, she hoped, at least as much self-confidence as she could see in him.

He had dragged out one of the kitchen chairs and was straddling it, resting his arms across the back of it and regarding her with a wary amusement that she found incredibly provoking. 'Hospitality isn't your long suit, is it?' he asked, lifting a dark eyebrow at her rigid posture, arms folded tightly across her chest.

'And gentlemanly behaviour isn't yours,' she countered acerbically.

'Are you referring to my past transgressions or those you imagine you're being subjected to presently?' he asked in the same teasing tone.

'I am referring to your insistence on discussing an event in our lives that would be better left forgotten.'

'*I* wasn't the one who brought it up.'

Torey's lips set in a thin line. 'I know. My mistake. I should never have alluded to my ridiculous infatuation. I did it only to point out to you that you needn't try to seduce me, that I have seen the error of my ways, and I have no intention of falling into bed with any shallow bedhopper who thinks the lonely widow might appreciate a lusty little romp.'

'Bully for you,' Jake said scathingly. 'Pardon me if I remain a bit sceptical.'

'What do you mean by that?'

'I think the lady protests too much.'

Torey glared. 'You would think that. I have met some colossal egos in my time, but yours takes the cake. Seven years ago you couldn't understand any girl who wouldn't immediately fall down on the sand and make love with you—there had to be something wrong with her—and now you think there's something wrong with me because I haven't flown out here from Illinois and promptly fallen into your bed!'

'Seven years ago I understood that you were a frightened, naïve little country girl who couldn't have made first team on the softball squad and who was suddenly playing in the big leagues . . .' Jake began, and the colour flared in Torey's cheeks.

'Oh!'

'So I made allowances,' he went on as though he hadn't heard her squeak of indignation. 'It might surprise you to know it, but even then I preferred a willing partner in bed. Now . . .' he shrugged, 'now I don't know what your problem is. Maybe it's a crime in northern Illinois to want to go to bed with someone and say so—I suppose it might be—but out here it's a way of saying I find you to be an attractive woman.'

'Is that what it is?' Torey asked with false sweetness as soon as she could find her voice again. A way of telling a woman she was attractive, indeed! What did he do if he thought they were beautiful, rip off their clothes?

'That's what it is,' Jake said flatly.

'Then, thank you for the compliment, kind sir. I'll try not to misunderstand next time,' she said sarcastically.

Jake kicked aside the chair and stood up, coming across the kitchen to stand in front of her. Looming, she thought. This is what they mean when they say someone is 'looming over you'. His eyes were like quicksilver. 'Feel free to take it literally, too,' he growled, and a split second later his arms went around her and his head dipped to brand her lips with his own.

'Jake!' It was a muffled cry, half shock, half panic. She struggled in his arms, fighting the heady promise of his kiss at the same time that she felt a prick of curiosity. A treacherous sliver of her wanted desperately to kiss him back. 'Damn it, Jake! No! Stop it!' She shoved against his chest, and finally he eased his grip on her, letting her break their embrace.

'Well,' he murmured, his breathing rough and slightly unsteady, 'what do you think now?'

'I think you'd better learn to take no for an answer,' she said frostily, turning her back on him and walking to the other side of the kitchen. She needed that table between them. She wished she could find another one to put between her rational mind and the emotions he had begun to evoke in her again.

Jake gave a short, harsh laugh. 'So much for growing up.' He shrugged and opened the back door, pausing only to say, 'Let me know when you change your mind. You might've been smarter at eighteen than now. I think we might have something here.'

What they had, Torey decided during the long night hours she spent staring at the dark ceiling of her bedroom, was a mess. She was supposed to be eliminating unwanted complications from her life by coming to California, not adding to them! She had been expecting a respite from the constant stream of men her family was urging in her direction, and she had expected to have no problem resisting the garden variety male transplanted to California. While she could now face the prospect of meeting a man whom she might one day come to love as she had Paul (a prospect that hadn't seemed possible until recently), she didn't for a moment think a fast lane Casanova would be that man. And if somewhere in the back of her mind she had wanted to run across Jake Brosnan again, it was once and for all to put him behind her. How humiliating to discover that she still found him attractive! Damn!

Groaning, she flipped over on the narrow bed and pressed her cheek against the cool dampness of the plaster wall. Through the window she could hear the surf pounding, bringing with it memories of that earlier summer when she would have given her most prized possession for the amount of attention that Jake had paid her tonight.

'Smarter at eighteen, ha!' she muttered aloud in the

stillness of the room. At eighteen she had been bewitched by a sexy grin, silky thick black hair, and stunning blue eyes. His brooding intensity one minute balanced against a devil-may-care impetuosity the next intrigued and attracted her. What she didn't know about him (and it was boundless) she could invent, and did. But the Jake she encountered on their fateful day failed to measure up to the hero of her dreams. So much for instant attraction, she thought, shifting restlessly again. How much more satisfying her relationship with Paul had been.

She smiled slightly, thinking of Paul with a fondness that she couldn't imagine ever feeling about someone as provoking as Jake. Some day maybe someone would come along who would fill her life the way Paul had, someone she could trust, share her hopes and dreams with, count on. And she would find him, she was sure, the way she found Paul—slowly, comfortably, easily. And they would know—as she and Paul had—that, sooner or later they were meant for each other. She sighed and closed her eyes thinking reluctantly, meanwhile there's Jake Brosnan to deal with.

The ringing 'phone woke her. How long it had been shrilling was debatable, but the frantic sound of her mother's voice when she finally answered made Torey think that it must have been quite a while.

'Are you all right?' her mother demanded.

'Fine,' Torey mumbled, prying her eyes open and reaching over to open the back door and let Maynard out into the yard. The sun was streaming in, making patterns on the linoleum.

'I thought you'd been mugged! Kidnapped!'

'Nooo . . .' Torey managed, still trying to focus in the bright midmorning light.

'What happened?'

Torey's brow furrowed. 'To what?'

'Heavens, Torey, you sound like you've been drugged.'

Torey laughed. 'No, I'm just waking up.'

'It's nearly noon!'

Torey squinted at the clock. 'Not here.'

'Well, even so, you should be up.' Her mother sounded annoyed, and Torey thought the shoe ought to be on the other foot. Who woke whom up after all?

'Did you want something?' she asked politely.

'To know you got there. I thought you'd call.'

Torey rolled her eyes. When would her mother realise she was an adult? She managed a non-committal grunt that must have appeased her mother, for the next words she heard were,

'What'd you think of Jake? Is he as gorgeous as Gran says?'

Torey straightened up immediately. Since when had Gran said Jake was gorgeous? All anyone had said to her about Jake was that he would be wearing a red shirt. More plotting afoot no doubt. Gran had probably said, 'I've got just the man for her,' and Mother had let Torey volunteer to take care of Gran like it was all her own idea. She wanted to grind her teeth. And what a man, for heaven's sake! If only they knew what they had done! 'If you like that type,' she said flatly, the implication being that she didn't.

'Oh.' Her mother sounded disappointed, but brightened quickly, saying, 'Well, it doesn't matter. I saw Peggy Lawson at the supermarket yesterday, and I mentioned you were in LA and she said their nephew Adam lived in Torrance, and I . . .'

'Mother!' Torey wailed. 'You didn't!'

'Well, I'm sure any nephew of Tom and Peggy Lawson is a very nice young man,' her mother said defensively.

They all were. Even Vince and Harlan were nice young men. But they weren't Paul. And she didn't need people finding her men, thank you very much. When she wanted to, she could find her own. Anyway, she had quite enough on her plate just dealing with Jake Brosnan, and she didn't know now whose fault he was—her grandmother's or her own.

'Well, I gave your address to Peggy,' Torey's mother went on. 'So you might hear from this Adam . . .'

'Terrific,' Torey muttered. 'I have to go now, Mom. There's someone at the door.'

A lie, she thought. But a small one. But no sooner had she said it than it was true. In fact it was worse than true, for one second there was a shadow on the back porch and the next Jake was opening the door and stepping into the room.

'Go away,' she hissed, wrapping her thin nightgown more tightly around her until she realised that it was even more provocative that way than if she left it hanging loose. 'I'll talk to you later in the week, Mother.'

'Who is it, dear? Don't let in strangers.'

'I'll try not to,' Torey said, hopping self-consciously from one foot to the other wishing herself invisible. Jake was looking at her figure silhouetted through the pale yellow gown with a hunger that suggested that he hadn't eaten in weeks.

'Stop it,' she said to him, and her mother demanded. 'Who is it, dear?'

'Mr Brosnan, Gran's tenant,' Torey said, trying to inject a little formality into the situation with minimal success because Jake was grinning at her, all tanned and sexy, with far too much bare skin showing for her liking. He wore only a pair of faded denim cut-offs, low-slung and hip-hugging, and she couldn't decide who she would most like to put her bathrobe on—him or herself!

'Oh, let me speak to him, dear,' her mother said in a breathless, fluttery tone that Torey didn't like at all. It smacked too much of the noises her mother made around Vince Liebfried.

'He doesn't want to talk to you now, Mom,' Torey began, only to have the 'phone wrenched from her grasp. 'Jake!'

'Oh, but I do,' he said blithely, holding her at arm's length while she flailed at him ineffectually. 'Mrs Stuart, isn't it?' he said into the 'phone, dodging Torey's kick. 'Yes, yes she is,' he said grinning. 'Every bit as lovely as Addie said she was . . .'

'Oooh!' Torey grabbed a dish towel and flicked it at him, hitting his rear end.

'I'll be happy to keep an eye on her, Mrs Stuart,' Jake went on, moving out of range of the dish towel. His eyes roved over Torey so blatantly that she felt as though he was touching her. She strongly doubted that even her matchmaking mother meant 'keeping an eye on' as literally as that. Flinging the dish towel into his smirking face, she flounced out of the room and banged her bedroom door with a ferocity that made the windows rattle. Wretch! she fumed, grabbing the nearest pair of jeans and a scoop-necked eyelet blouse that would, she hoped, cool her off. Between her mother and Jake the morning had certainly got off to a smashing start. If Jake didn't know he was being served up as matrimonial material before, he certainly knew it now. And if that wasn't enough, her mother had tossed in someone called Adam for good measure. God, even California wasn't going to be far enough away apparently. She wanted to scream.

Glancing at the mirror she wondered momentarily what Jake had seen that was worth hungering for. Dark hair cascaded in a dishevelled tangle almost to her waist. Her face, completely devoid of any make-up, was pale. Only her deep green eyes might possibly be conceived of as very attractive—and a man would have to be very hungry indeed, she thought, to overlook the rest and settle on those. She tugged a brush resolutely through the snarls, finally plaiting it and pinning it in one long plait in a coil on top of her head. It was an improvement all right. She looked much more in control of the situation now—if not regal and detached, at least competent and non-hysterical. Much more capable of dealing with the presence of Jake Brosnan.

A good thing, too, for at that moment Jake tapped on the door and opened it before she could utter a sound. 'Your mother sends her love,' he said, the grin still lurking on his face.

Torey rolled her eyes. 'That's not all she sent, believe me.'

'Well, no, you're right. It's not.' He came in and shut the door, moving across the room with catlike grace to stand in front of her. Tipping her chin up and looking into her wide green eyes, he murmured, 'She also sent this,' and his lips touched hers, gently at first. A motherly kiss, Torey thought bemused and a tiny bit pleased with herself for standing up under it so passively. But almost imperceptibly the kiss changed, deepened, sought an entrance that she could not deny. His tongue probed, tasted, stroked against her own, and Torey felt herself slipping. She grabbed for his shirt front and encountered only a bare, hair-roughened chest, hard and muscular beneath her fingers.

'J-Jake?' she stammered, wondering where all that self-control she was so proud of had gone.

'Hmmmmm?' The kiss ended as slowly as it had begun, and Jake stepped back and cocked his head quizzically. 'And what does she usually send?' he asked hoarsely.

'Men.' Torey could barely say the word. Her voice was no more than a breathless whisper. Snap out of it, she commanded herself. A kiss is a kiss. Even Vince Liebfried kisses. But not like that! she couldn't help but think.

Jake shook his head, chuckling softly. 'She doesn't need to,' he said. 'Not when she's got me on the spot.'

'As far as I'm concerned you're not on the spot,' Torey said, silently congratulating herself for having got her feet back on the ground once more. She moved quickly towards the door, anxious to get away from the intimacy of her bedroom. 'I'm about to fix breakfast. I suppose you've already eaten,' she said hopefully.

'I fed Scott,' he answered, following her into the kitchen with the tenacity of Maynard when he thought a can of dog food might be in the offing. 'But I could stand more than cornflakes myself.'

'What did you have in mind?' she said ungraciously, and Jake grinned, making her remember his comment about her lack of hospitality last night. He was obviously recalling it too.

'An omelette, maybe,' he said. 'There are mushrooms and cheese in the fridge. Also some bacon?' He looked at her hopefully. If he had a tail he'd wag it, she thought glumly.

'I suppose.'

'Great. How about a swim first?'

'What?'

'Let's go for a swim before breakfast. Good for the appetite.'

Torey gave him a hard stare. 'You already have a good appetite.'

'A man has many hungers,' Jake said easily, a teasing light in his eyes. 'A nice cold swim might assuage a couple of mine.'

'By all means, let's swim then,' Torey said sarcastically. 'I'll meet you down there.'

'I don't mind waiting while you change,' he said, and dropped into one of the oak, spindle back chairs, stretching his feet out in front of him, crossing them at the ankle. 'Hurry up, though.'

Torey made strangling motions with her hands. Damn him, why didn't he just leave? Then she could bolt the door and have a nice, quiet breakfast in peace—alone. 'Hurry up, though,' she fumed as she rummaged through her suitcase and came up with a serviceable but hardly elegant two piece swimsuit. Serve him right, she thought, stripping off her jeans and blouse. Used to the all but non-existent bikinis that dotted the beaches of southern California, Jake would doubtless find her modest suit, appropriate though it was for swimming in Apple River Canyon or at the 'Y' in Dubuque, to be a joke here. Perhaps, she thought, hooking the bra and gazing critically at the vivid blue and green floral pattern of the suit, it will stun him so much that he will go off me altogether! She could but hope.

'Nice,' Jake said when she reappeared, and he didn't look put off at all.

Keep your eyes to yourself, she thought, hastily wrapping a bath sheet around herself sarong fashion. 'After you,' she said, and followed him out the door.

'Where's Scott?' she asked, catching up to him as he opened the gate and waited for her to go out.

'Playing at a friend's. I've had to make other arrangements since Addie's been gone.'

Torey bristled slightly. 'She's your babysitter?'

'Yeah. Most mornings anyway. Usually she fed him breakfast, too.' He didn't seem at all reticent about discussing it.

'Must be nice for you,' Torey said shortly. Sleeping in after hard nights, recovering from hangovers in peace. Seven years ago that sort of behaviour had been confined to weekends because he had had to be at the ad agency the rest of the time. Now, apparently, he could carouse all week.

'Suits us both,' Jake said amiably, and nodded in greeting to a couple of young women in bathing suits who were roller skating along The Strand.

'Coming again Saturday night, honey?' the blonde one asked him as she whizzed past.

Jake grinned. 'Of course, I'm a fixture. You know that.'

'I'll be looking for you,' she called over her shoulder and blew him a kiss.

Torey looked at him sourly. 'Friends of yours?' she asked trying to keep from wrinkling her nose and attempting a casualness she was far from feeling. Why couldn't she just feel supreme disinterest where Jake Brosnan was concerned?

'Acquaintances,' Jake said easily as he stepped over the low wall to the sandy beach and offered her a hand. She took it, wishing that his touch didn't sear her.

Shades of adolescence, she chided herself, and withdrew her hand immediately when she got her footing in the sand. Jake quirked an eyebrow but didn't say a word. Damn, why had she told him that she had had a crush on him? Now he would be interpreting her every move in light of that juvenile infatuation.

The sand was barely warm underfoot now, but by mid-afternoon she knew it would be so hot she would want to wear thongs. Now it was comfortably gritty and soft between her toes. Jake was striding on ahead, and she couldn't help feasting her eyes on him, watching the play of the morning sun across the tanned expanse of his back, the way the towel slung around his neck ruffled up the hair on the back of his head. He was still every bit the virile male animal she had known seven years ago—and, she thought grimly, still as attractive as ever to the opposite sex. Those two women on roller skates—hardly more than girls really—had been the only women they had met and Jake had known them. Probably he knew thousands. Seven years and a five-year-old son hadn't slowed him down any! Not when he had Addie to babysit for him too.

Jake stopped just before the high tide mark and dropped his towel. 'Suit you?' he asked, turning to watch her cross the sand towards him.

'It's fine.' She laid her towel out carefully and was about to sit down, when Jake said.

'I thought we were going swimming.' His hand went to the fastener of his cut-off jeans and, mesmerised, she watched as he slid down the zipper and the faded blue denim slithered down his hips leaving only equally worn, formerly navy blue trunks in their place.

She had been going to say, 'I'm not hot enough yet,' but suddenly she was burning. She turned and darted past him, running towards the breakers, hoping to drown once and for all the desire she felt. Splashing through the surf, she dived under the first wave, shattered, then numbed by the cold water on her burning skin. She came up gasping to be slapped in the face by an oncoming wave. Bobbing to the surface, she struck out in a head-up breast stroke due west putting, she hoped, plenty of green water between herself and Jake Brosnan.

Swimming was wonderful, exhilarating, like a sudden rebirth after months of being overwhelmed by the petty concerns and worries of everyday life. God, how much she had forgotten! She laughed aloud feeling the power of the water surging beneath her as an unbroken wave rolled in towards the shore. Out beyond even the surfers now, she turned back, expecting to see Jake's dark head bobbing amidst the waves far behind her. Instead he was scarcely six feet from her, the black hair plastered to his forehead, a fierce scowl on his face.

'You're out too far, Torey,' he growled. 'Come on back, now.' He looked like he was biting back several more things he would rather have said to her, and Torey stared, remembering the daredevil surfer she had known as J.B. The satisfied smile slipped from her face.

'Come on.' He was adamant, and from the look of him she thought he might knock her out and drag her shoreward if she didn't turn back, so she obediently began to paddle towards the beach, letting the incoming surf do much of the work for her.

'I thought you wanted to swim,' she said as they moved along side by side through the glassy water.

'Not to China.' His voice was still gruff but some of the tension seemed to have eased. 'It's been a long time since you've been in the ocean,' he said, obviously feeling a need to explain his demand that she return.

'Yes, but I still swim a lot. Paul and I went to the "Y" in Dubuque a couple of times a week. I kept it up. I used to swim a mile every time I went. You needn't have worried.'

He made a wry face and flicked a wet strand of hair out of his eyes. 'Maybe. But it shocked me to see you take off like that. I thought it might be a burst of girlish enthusiasm or . . .' his voice trailed off and she replied curtly,

'I told you, I've grown up. Bursts of girlish enthusiasm—*all kinds* of girlish enthusiasm—are a thing of the past.'

Air whistled slowly through Jake's teeth and a grim look flickered over his rugged features. 'So you said,' he muttered, and glancing over his shoulder, he said, 'Here comes one.' Before she could make a move, he had dipped his head and taken two powerful strokes, fitting himself neatly into the flow of the wave and, while she bobbed helplessly above it, he shot away, his body dropping over the crest and surging along with the breaker until he stood up far away in knee deep water and shook his wet hair. He walked straight up the beach to their towels and dropped down face first never once looking back.

Torey stared after him, puzzled, caught in a riptide of emotions. Jake blew hot and cold, infuriated her and attracted her, chased her and then swam away. Which one was the real Jake? Or were any of them? And why did she care? There was no more future in being interested in Jake Brosnan now than there had been seven years ago. He would only want now what he had wanted then—a one-night stand, a warm bed, some good sex. It certainly wouldn't be called 'making love'. She doubted Jake even knew what real love was.

He had rolled over on to his back now and was raised up on his elbows and forearms, squinting out at the waves looking for her. He probably thinks I've drowned, Torey thought and began swimming towards the shore, not wanting him to come out to 'rescue' her again. She had more trouble than Jake had catching a wave, but at last caught a small one, enjoying the sensation of being rushed along until her knees scraped the sand.

Adjusting the top of her suit while she was still face down in the water, she recalled a time that previous summer when she'd lost it entirely. She had swum back out beyond the breakers, helpless and embarrassed, until Mick had taken pity on her and had brought her out a towel, draping it around her shoulders and fending off the teasing comments as he walked her back to her grandmother's house. Mick had been kind, gentle, comfortable. Not at all, she thought, like Jake.

She walked back up the beach towards him, ignoring his stare until she reached the edge of her towel. He reached over and handed it to her wordlessly. She dried off, self-conscious, aware of his eyes following the towel as she dried her long, slim legs, flat stomach and pale arms. 'I was wondering,' she began, more to divert his attention from her body than because she wanted to know, 'whatever became of Mick?'

Pain flickered across Jake's face and his stomach muscles clenched. 'Mick?' he said hollowly. Then, 'Mick's dead.' His eyes closed and, with a move as definite as shutting a door in her face, he rolled over on to his stomach and, cradling his head in his arms facing away from her, Jake lay perfectly still.

CHAPTER FOUR

'What happened?'

She knew just by looking at him that he didn't want to talk about it, but she couldn't stop herself from asking. Mick? Dead? It didn't seem possible. She could still see him as clearly as if he had only just walked down the beach with his surfboard balanced easily on top of his sunbleached blond head. She could remember well a young man with an engaging grin, one chipped tooth right in front, and a perennially sunburned nose centred below two startlingly blue eyes. She blinked and looked over at Jake again. He was getting up to his knees slowly, not looking at her.

'He was surfing.' Jake's voice was toneless. He shut his eyes against the pain but his voice betrayed none of the emotion she saw momentarily on his face. 'He drowned.'

Cold settled over Torey like a shroud. She felt chilled to the bone, numb, like she had when Paul died. 'Oh Jake, I'm sorry. So sorry.' She knew it was inadequate, but she wanted to reach out to him, offer him a crumb of comfort at the loss of his good friend. But Jake had closed up. There was no other way to describe it, she thought. His face had become an unreadable blank; he sat back on his heels, absolutely still, a waxen reproduction of his real self. Finally he drew a long, harsh breath.

'Yes,' he said roughly after a moment's hesitation as though he didn't wholly trust his voice. 'I'm sorry, too.' He got to his feet and swiped the towel across his sandy, hair-roughened legs. 'I'm ready for that omelette now. How about you?'

Torey stared, confused, as he turned and walked

back up the beach. She was still dealing with Mick's
death and he was talking about breakfast! 'Jake! Wait!'
She scrambled to her feet and ran after him.

'What?' He looked back at her, eyes wary, feet still
moving in the direction of the house.

'I—I'm hungry too,' she faltered. She had intended to
ask, 'When did it happen? How?' but his face stopped
her. She knew quite clearly that it wasn't breakfast he
was interested in; it was simply that he couldn't talk any
more about Mick. Maybe it had been too recent, or
maybe he just hadn't resolved it in his mind. For a long
time she had broken down every single time she talked
about Paul. But she knew that eventually, by talking
about him and working her feelings through, that she'd
be able to remember him with love and happiness and
not only with tears. So she had talked, *ad nauseum* she
sometimes thought, to her parents, siblings, Paul's
family, their friends, anyone who would listen for that
matter. And slowly she had accepted Paul's death, had
accepted his place in her life. Now she longed to share
some of that acceptance with Jake. He looked so tense,
so awkward, like a hunted animal caught in the sight of
a powerful gun. Gently, almost unthinkingly, she smiled
at him and reached for his hand.

No words passed between them as they made their
way back to the house, Jake's hand clasped loosely in
hers. Torey felt the warm roughness of his hand in hers
and marvelled at her daring in reaching out to him and
felt inordinately pleased that, for once, he made no
move to press for more. Rather he seemed willing to
accept only what closeness she was willing to give. He
matched his stride to hers, his shoulder brushing
against hers as they walked with an easiness that was,
she realised, a far cry from their tension filled walk along
The Strand on their ill-fated date seven years ago. This
was more like her fantasies. This Jake was more the
man she'd dreamed of—a thoughtful man, caring, and
even vulnerable.

Watch out, Torey Cooper, she told herself. Watch out.

'Go get changed,' Jake said as they entered the kitchen. 'I'll start the eggs.' He had loosed his hand from hers to unlock the door, but she still felt a bond, a closeness that made her linger unwilling to relinquish this very real rapport she felt with him. She hovered in the hallway watching him remove a carton of eggs from the refrigerator and go back for the mushrooms, cheese and bacon. An urge to touch him again nearly overwhelmed her as her eyes traced the line of his shoulders, ran down the length of his spine from the damp, spiky hair on his neck to the low rise of his worn, faded swim trunks.

Jake turned to reach for an onion and caught her staring. Colour ran up into her cheeks and she shifted her gaze uncomfortably. 'Trying to figure out what you ever saw in me?' Jake grinned, and Torey couldn't help smiling back.

'It is a bit puzzling,' she teased, then fled to the bedroom to change back into her jeans and blouse before she betrayed any more of the desire she felt.

'I hope you figure it out,' Jake called after her.

Torey didn't know what she hoped. She shut the door to her bedroom quietly and padded over to the dresser, stripping off the wet suit as she went. Her picture of Paul leaning against the oak tree in their back yard smiled up at her. 'Oh Paul,' she whispered, 'what am I doing?' But her 5 × 7 Paul just grinned, amused and indulgent, not helpful at all. 'He's not like you, Paul,' she told the picture as she dressed. With Paul there had been no surprises, no tensions, no question that their love had been the right thing. It was all so reasonable, so sensible. She had known him for years. They had been friends in school, had swam together, hiked together, milked cows together, gone to dances together. Their relationship had developed slowly—first as friends, then in college as a couple. If Paul had had any doubts, he never expressed them. And Torey's had been confined to her eighteenth summer—the months she had spent in California when she thought the sun rose and set on J.B. Proof that it didn't—that J.B. was no more the romantic, tender hero than any of the other here-today-gone-tomorrow types that populated much of the beachfront—was all Torey needed once she got home in the autumn to fall into the easy companionship and slowly blossoming passion that she felt with Paul Cooper. And things had worked out. They had had a good marriage by anyone's standards. Lots of love, laughter and caring, passion and tenderness. She had had it all. Now, looking at Paul, she knew that she didn't want to spend the rest of her life without it.

She set the photo back on the dresser and began towelling her hair dry. Perhaps, she thought for the first time since Paul died, her mother might be right after all. Maybe she did need to meet men—calm, sensible, caring men like Paul. She couldn't go through life as an empty shell, living on past memories, loving past loves. It left her hollow, barren—and far too susceptible to the likes of Jake Brosnan. He had only to look at her and frissons of awareness danced along her spine. It shouldn't be that way.

And it wouldn't be, she decided if she made an effort to let other men into her life. This Adam, Peggy's nephew, for instance. I almost hope he does call, she thought as she pulled a brush through the tangle of long dark hair still damp against her back. Maybe he's just what I need. And what's that? she asked herself severely. The answer was obvious—an antidote to Jake Brosnan.

'Omelette's done,' he hollered, and she gave up trying to do anything constructive with her hair and simply pulled it back at the nape of her neck and knotted a bright yellow scarf around it.

Jake had set the table, and she found a fluffy cheese

omelette with bacon and sautéd mushrooms at her place. He held her chair for her with the elegance of a white-coated waiter in a four-star restaurant, and then went around to sit across from her, still clad only in bathing trunks. Embarrassed by his gesture of politeness, Torey said,

'I think you need a tie in this establishment.' Jake grinned and wrapped the dish towel around his neck.

'How's this?'

'It'll do,' she said, reaching across to straighten it. 'But it would look nicer if you'd wear it so Gran's embroidered cardinal wasn't inside out.' Her fingers brushed his chest and Jake dipped his head to look at them, and Torey thought that touching him hadn't been a good idea at all. She snatched her hand back quickly and buttered a piece of bread with fierce concentration.

'It's good bread,' she told him through a mouthful, hoping to find a neutral subject. 'Is it from the bakery up the hill?'

'Brosnan's Bakery,' Jake told her as he forked some omelette into his mouth.

'*You* made it?'

He shrugged. 'My creativity is not confined totally to pencil and paper.'

'I didn't imagine it was,' she retorted, her thoughts skipping instantly to Scott. She could tell from the sardonic glance he gave her that his thoughts had followed, and fumbling, she went on, 'What are you working on now? What book, I mean?' Her cheeks went scarlet, but Jake chose to take the question as it had been intended.

'Would you believe, dragons?'

'Dragons?' His earlier books, she recalled, had been mostly water-colour and pen-and-ink realistic or folk tales. Many were set at the seashore. The fierce, fire-breathing boldness of dragons didn't seem to fit.

'Yep. Not my usual job.'

'What made you take it then?'

'Scott, I guess. He liked the story. There's this dragon who's looking for a mother . . .' Jake's mouth twisted wryly. 'You can guess why he likes it.' His head bent over his plate and Torey saw a new rigidity in his shoulders.

'Does Scott miss his mother a lot?'

Jake grimaced. 'Hardly. He hasn't seen her for over two years. She's not exactly a doting mother. It's *having* a mother that he misses I think. Any mother.' Jake rubbed a hand against the back of his neck. 'He brings me home a lot of potential ones to interview, believe me! He's a lot like your mother in that respect!'

Torey laughed, but her heart hurt for Scott. What kind of mother would just go off and leave her child? Or couldn't she stand being married to Jake? Torey paused, forkful of omelette halfway to her mouth, and knew that she wouldn't want to be married to a man whose eye roved as easily and continually as Jake's did. Maybe his ex-wife hadn't either. But it wasn't the sort of thing she could ask. She was overwhelmingly glad when the 'phone rang and she was saved from replying at all.

'It's probably Addie,' Jake speculated, 'wondering when we're coming to get her.'

But it wasn't. When she picked up the 'phone Torey heard a masculine voice. 'Is this Torey Cooper? It's Gino Martinelli here,' the voice said. 'You remember? Francesca's brother.'

'Of course!' Torey beamed. Francesca was the one close friend she had made that earlier summer, the only one she had let know she was coming back. Gino was her older brother, a muscular blond Viking with an unlikely Italian name. He would have been high on Torey's list of eligible men if she hadn't been besotted with J.B. 'How are you, Gino?'

'Great. But Francesca and family have moved to Berkeley. When she got your letter she suggested that I give you a call. How about dinner on Friday?'

Taken aback by the suddenness of it, Torey looked up and stared at Jake. He scowled at her. Perversely her heart speeded up, and she took a deep breath trying to calm it. 'I'd love to, Gino,' she said hastily. 'See you then.'

Jake got to his feet and began thumping the breakfast dishes in the sink. Torey hung up and offered, 'I'll do those.'

Jake snorted. 'Who's Gino?' he demanded, his back to her.

'An old friend.'

'Someone you knew seven years ago?'

'Yes.'

'I thought you didn't hop into bed with every man you met,' he growled. 'Or did you make an exception just for me?'

'Gino never expected me to hop into bed with him,' she said flatly. 'That was only a prerequisite for playing in your league. Remember?'

'Don't be smart. I didn't go to bed with every girl I took out in those days.'

'No, just every one but me.'

Jake's teeth snapped together. 'Regretting it now?' he mocked.

'Like hell! The only thing I regret is having run into you again at all. 'You haven't changed a bit, have you?'

Jake grinned infuriatingly. 'You'll never find out if you don't try, will you?'

Torey slammed her coffee cup on the table, sloshing the hot liquid all over the chequered cloth. 'I'll survive without knowing, thank-you very much. You told me once to go home and grow up before I tried your league again. Well, listen to me, Mr Brosnan, I've been home and I've grown up, and surprisingly enough I learned something in the process: I don't *want* to play ball in your league!' Her voice rose, shaking with emotion. 'It can't compare to what I found with Paul! Not ever!' Spinning around, she ran from the kitchen and slammed the door to her bedroom, flinging herself on her bed while dry sobs wracked her.

God, I am an idiot, she thought rolling over and studying the ceiling in despair. For two years I have lived a sane, mature, controlled, well-ordered existence on my own, and within 24 hours of meeting up again with Jake Brosnan, I am screaming like a banshee, sobbing like an adolescent, and aching like a sex-starved maniac. What am I going to do?

She heard the back door close quietly and lifted the curtain a fraction to see Jake crossing the backyard. He bent to pat Maynard before mounting the stairs to his apartment. Looking at him objectively—if that was indeed possible, she thought wryly—it was easy enough to figure out what she had once seen in him. He was a handsome man with all that black hair and those blue eyes, that well-muscled physique and the sexy grin. And besides the tangibles, she acknowledged ruefully, there was an intensity about him, a drive, a bottled-up energy that compelled her with the same force that the surging wave had swept her along that very morning. If she didn't start learning to swim where Jake was concerned she was in danger of being swept away. And she didn't want that—not at all. She watched as Jake turned and gazed back at Gran's house for a moment, a rather bleak expression on his face. He didn't much look like he was thrilled with her either.

Probably wonders what he's got himself into, Torey thought, dropping the curtain slowly and stretching back out on the bed. There was no question that he was attracted to her physically now. But she doubted that he had any real intention of being served up as a marriage prospect by her grandmother. She smiled slightly. He'd be walking a tightrope where Addie-the-matchmaker was concerned! He'd probably be grateful if she did find an interest elsewhere. And once she discovered that she wasn't just going to hang about like a ripe plum waiting to be plucked, she had no doubt that he would waste little time on her. Without question there were plenty of women around who would love to be a feast for him. But not Torey. No, very definitely not her.

Tell that to Gran, she thought ruefully a few hours later when, while Jake was trudging back out to the pick-up to bring in another load of Gran's things, her grandmother had plumped herself up further on her pillows and asked, 'What do you think of him?'

No question who *him* was. Torey hung her grandmother's robe in the closet. 'He's, um, nice.'

Gran snorted. 'Nice? Puppies are nice. Chicken soup is nice. Shawls are nice . . .'

'You're right,' Torey said abruptly. 'He's not nice at all.'

Gran looked satisfied with that. 'I told your mother . . .' she began, and Torey gnashed her teeth.

'I can find my own men, Gran!' she protested.

'I'm sure you can, dear,' Gran agreed complacently. 'But your mother said you weren't overly interested in Vince or Marlon . . .'

'Harlan.'

'Whoever,' Gran nodded, smoothing the bedcover. 'So I just thought you ought to know who else is available.'

'You make it sound like window shopping!' Torey laughed.

'Nothing wrong with that,' her grandmother said. 'It's where I got your grandfather, out of a window. Dressing manikins he was, and I was looking for a new spring coat. Got him instead.'

Torey stared. 'I never knew that.'

Gran lifted her shoulders. 'Lots you don't know,' she said enigmatically. 'But there's nothing wrong with a bit of window shopping, Victoria. At least it means you've got your eyes open again.'

Too true, Torey thought. And at that moment they

were filled with the sight of Jake, staggering into the bedroom under the load of two suitcases, a portable hairdryer and a birdcage.

'My God, Addie,' he gasped, letting the suitcases slip from his arms as Torey rescued the canary, 'next time hire a moving company. I thought I was bringing home a little old lady, not taking a crash course in training for a job with North American Van Lines.'

'Poor Jake,' Addie clucked sympathetically. 'Victoria will get you a beer.'

Jake looked sceptical, as though he doubted Torey would do much more than haggle with him or scream at him if her past behaviour was anything to go by. They had existed in an uneasy truce since he came to get her that afternoon. At first Scott had been in the truck, his chatter making a welcome barrier which neither of them crossed. But once he had been dropped off at kindergarten, the silence lay like an ocean between them. Finally, during a particularly long wait at a stop light, Jake had cleared his throat and muttered, 'Sorry.'

Torey looked over at him, amazed. 'Sorry?'

He shrugged. 'I seem to irritate you without even trying.'

How perceptive of him. 'It's partly my fault,' she acknowledged. It was mostly her fault, to be frank. He could have no idea of the disruptive effect he still had on her even after all these years. But she couldn't quite accept that he wasn't *trying* to annoy her—she wasn't the one doing the baiting, after all.

The light changed and he eased the truck into the intersection, waiting patiently to make a left turn. 'Truce?' he asked.

Torey's eyes flickered down the length of him, still seeing the firmly muscled body on the beach beneath his blue jeans and open-necked blue sports shirt. A retreat seemed more sensible—clear back to Illinois— judging from what just looking at him did to her. But then she remembered Vince and Harlan, and knew she couldn't go back at all. 'Truce,' she agreed, and he nodded, apparently satisfied.

But he was surprised when she handed him the beer and even more so when she made them all sandwiches unasked.

'Ground glass, is it?' he said, taking it suspiciously.

'And let my grandmother know what I really think of you?'

Jake made a face. 'You're doing this for Addie?'

'Of course.'

'You'll give her ideas,' he warned.

It was possible, Torey acknowledged. Addie would think that her matchmaking efforts were not all in vain. But she was counting on Jake to squelch that. All he wanted was to go to bed with her. She would keep him out of bed. Let him convince Addie that marriage wasn't on his mind. 'I'll take my chances,' she said, and left him chewing his tuna sandwich thoughtfully while she got Addie another cup of tea.

CHAPTER FIVE

ADDIE was too exhausted from her move back home to do more than make them wash dishes together the first night. But Torey thought her grandmother was going to be a formidable pest when she felt up to par. She spent every waking moment extolling Jake's virtues until Torey began to think up excuses to go on errands alone. By Wednesday, all conceivable errands accomplished, she was ready to tear her hair. Addie had spent the entire morning alternately playing snap with Scott and telling Torey what a gem Scott's father was.

'Which war did you pick up your techniques in?' Torey asked finally, interrupting Addie's monologue about Jake's ability to diagnose and repair the ailments of her highly unpredictable car.

'What, dear?' Addie was driving one of Scott's jeeps across her quilt, trying to avoid the motorcycle policeman who was Scott.

'This brainwashing, Gran. Where'd you learn it?'

'Whatever do you mean, dear?' Addie asked, dodging the issue as successfully as she did Scott's motorcycle man. 'I'm just making conversation. Telling you about a good friend.'

Torey rolled her eyes. 'Who also happens to be "available" as you told me the other afternoon.'

'That, too,' Addie agreed, smiling beatifically. 'Goodness, Victoria, you are becoming very touchy.'

And she became touchier as the week wore on. She might have found Addie's enthusiasm amusing if she hadn't been the object of it—she and Jake. But she didn't. And Jake was no help at all. If she had expected him to resist Addie's matchmaking ploys, she was sadly mistaken. He was the one who was amused. And he seemed to see nothing wrong with going along with whatever scheme her grandmother concocted.

Torey lost no time in realising that however much her grandmother might, in fact, need her services as a physical therapist, Addie thought Torey needed a matchmaker more. And she had no hesitation about working in her scheme wherever there was an opening. Even during her exercises.

'Gran, that's enough,' Torey said as Addie raised her leg slowly.

Addie shook her head obstinately. 'Just a few more, Torey, dear. What's a few more?'

'Too many,' Torey said in exasperation. 'Because fifteen lifts are good for you, it doesn't stand to reason that thirty are twice as good.'

'It doesn't?' Addie didn't look convinced. 'What do you think, Jake?' she demanded of the man leaning against the fireplace and cradling a coffee mug in his hands.

A few days ago Torey would've dismissed him with a 'What does he know?' but the past week had taught her that what Jake thought was gospel. If Jake said fifteen was enough, Addie believed. If he didn't, God help the physical therapist who did. 'Jake?' she deferred to him sweetly, her eyes belying her honeyed tones.

'Better do what Torey says, Addie,' Jake advised, an unrepressed twinkle in his eyes. 'Torey's the boss.'

There's a laugh, Torey thought. Anyone with less control of a situation would be hard to find. She might know the proper sequence of exercises to help Addie develop her walking ability again, but she couldn't make Addie do them if she didn't want to. And Addie had turned into a tough bargainer. She seemed to think every five steps was a negotiating point.

'I'll walk tonight,' Addie would say, 'while you go out for a walk with Jake.'

'I don't want to go out for a walk with Jake,' Torey argued.

'Don't blame you,' Addie said complacently. 'I don't much want to walk between here and the sink either. But I will if you will.'

Fuming, Torey agreed. The next night, Thursday, it had been a bike ride to the Redondo Harbour. 'I'm too tired,' she groaned, and Addie nodded agreeably.

'Me, too,' her grandmother said, flexing her leg carefully. 'Think I'll just take it easy tonight. No exercises.'

'You need to,' Torey argued, annoyed as much by the grin that Jake wasn't hiding very successfully as by her grandmother's machinations.

'Of course you're right,' Addie said. 'I hate to be watched though. Just a little bike ride, hmm, Torey?'

'You shouldn't be left on your own.'

'Scott'll be here,' Addie reminded her. 'We can keep an eye on each other. And you can keep an eye on Jake.'

Which was exactly what she didn't want to do. Every minute she spent in Jake's presence was torture. She didn't want to want him but, damn it, she did. She had stayed out of his way as much as she could figuring that their 'truce' stood a better chance of surviving if it wasn't put to the test too often. But it didn't stop her thinking about him, fantasising about him, mooning about him like some lovesick teenager. It would have been faintly tolerable if he had been as indifferent to her as he had been seven years ago. Unfortunately that was not the case. He was positively encouraging her idiocy. And Addie wasn't helping matters at all.

Either she couldn't do anything unless Torey humoured her by going out with Jake while she did it, or she did too much in a misguided effort to get well immediately. Only Jake seemed to be able to convince her to slow down these efforts, and much as she resented having to do so, Torey bowed to his influence over her grandmother.

'I'll stop then,' Addie said, collapsing into her rocker,

'if you'll go to the end-of-the-year assembly at the PTA meeting with Jake tonight.'

'Can't,' Torey said immediately, wishing for a split second that she could have. Jake at a PTA meeting would have been worth seeing.

'What do you mean, you can't?' Addie demanded, her bright blue eyes boring into her granddaughter.

'I have a date,' Torey said smugly, tossing a silent thank you to Francesca.

'A date?' Addie sounded mortally offended.

'Isn't that the general idea?' Torey teased. 'That seems to be everyone in the family's main goal: find Torey a date. Well, I took pity on you all and found one of my own. So you can relax and stop trying to palm me off on Jake. I would appreciate it, and I'm sure he will.'

'I never!' Addie bristled. 'Have I ever forced you to take Torey out, Jake?' she demanded.

'Never,' Jake denied, lips twitching.

Torey shot him an irritated glance and got to her feet. 'Well, if you'll both excuse me I have to go and get ready.'

Jake gave her a mocking bow as she passed him and she barely contained a desire to kick his shin as she went by. 'Have a nice time tonight, Dad,' she said sweetly.

'I'm sure I will,' he lied genially. 'Pity you can't come. Scott would have liked it.'

That turned out to be an understatement. When Scott hurtled in from playing in the garden, Torey was just emerging from her room wearing a thin peasant blouse and a flowery wrap-around skirt, and he skidded to a stop in front of her and said, 'Boy, those kids'll really think you're somethin'.'

'Kids?' Torey was confused for a moment, then said, 'Oh, but Scott, I'm not going to your meeting. I have a date.'

Scott's face fell a mile. 'You aren't?' His voice was

hollow, crushed. He spun away from her and raced into the living room where Jake and Addie were talking. 'She isn't comin'!' he yelled.

'Scott . . .' Torey heard Jake's voice, gentle and weary.

'You said . . .' Scott accused, voice breaking.

'He didn't know she couldn't,' Addie put in, trying to smooth things over.

'He promised!' Scott wailed.

'Scott! Stop it!' Jake was angry now. 'I never promised you any such thing!'

'But . . .' Torey could hear the tears in his voice.

'I know,' Jake soothed, 'you want somebody besides me to come, don't you?' His tone was conciliatory now.

Scott sniffed. 'It's the last assembly of the year,' he mumbled. 'All the Moms and Dads come. Both of 'em.' His voice was heavy on *Moms* and *both*.

'Well, your mother isn't here,' Jake said flatly. 'And Torey can't come. How about . . .' he seemed to cast around for a suitable replacement. 'How about Auntie Lola?'

'I don' care,' Scott said sullenly.

'Well, don't do me any favours,' Jake said, exasperated.

'I wanted Torey,' Scott said stubbornly.

'I'm sorry, Scott,' Torey said then, coming into the room and kneeling beside the little boy, not looking up at his father. 'If I had known before I would have planned to come with you.'

Jake snorted sceptically. 'Like you planned to go bike riding,' he muttered darkly.

Torey glared fiercely at him. 'That is *not* the same thing at all. I would have liked to go to Scott's assembly.' She gave the little boy a hug and didn't even flinch when he rubbed a grimy fist against his tear-stained cheeks before hugging her neck. 'Another time?' she asked him, a hint of promise in her voice.

Scott sniffed again and nodded. 'Okay.'

'*You* invite me next time.'

'I will,' he promised. 'See,' he said triumphantly to his father, 'you shoulda let *me* ask her.'

Jake's teeth clenched. 'I—oh hell——' He glanced out the window. 'Your date's here,' he said tersely to Torey, and if she thought he muttered something about being saved by the bell, she couldn't be sure. She gave him a quick smile and hurried to open the door.

'Gino, how marvellous to see you!'

He did look marvellous too—even more the stunningly handsome Viking than she remembered. 'Torey, you did grow up!' He swung her into his arms, giving her a bear hug that blotted out almost all sensations except the distinct sound of Jake gritting his teeth.

'Gino,' she said when he set her back down, 'I'd like you to meet my grandmother, Mrs Harrison.'

Gino shook hands with Addie, giving her a warm, good-natured grin that seemed to erase the penetrating gaze that Addie had fixed him with at first.

'And this is Gran's tenant, Jake Brosnan,' Torey went on hurriedly, and stepped back as though she might get caught in the crossfire. Gino's blue eyes were warm and smiling; Jake's were chips of ice. It took him an eternity to accept the handshake that Gino offered, and Torey wanted to step on his foot. He was acting like a very suspicious father whose daughter was about to go out with a convicted rapist. 'And this is Jake's son, Scott,' she finished.

'You're Torey's date?' Scott was giving Gino an even more thorough inspection than Jake had.

'That's right.'

'I wanted her to come to my PTA meetin',' Scott said guilelessly.

'Scott!' Jake growled.

Gino pulled a face. 'Sorry, old man, if I'd known we could've worked something out.' He looked at Jake speculatively and then shrugged, slanting Torey a grin. 'Ready?'

'Yes.' Definitely, she thought. Not a second too soon. She plucked her shawl off the back of Gran's rocking-chair and bent to kiss her grandmother. 'See you in the morning,' she said.

'What makes you think I won't be up when you get in?' Addie asked, pecking her cheek.

'You'd better not be,' Torey laughed. 'You need your sleep. Jake will see that you behave yourself.' She tried to give him a comradely smile but he was staring stonily at her. 'Well, er, bye now,' she said, flustered at the look in his eyes, and practically bolted out the door ahead of Gino.

'He own you or something?' Gino asked as they walked up the hill to Manhattan Avenue where Gino had parked.

'Jake? No, of course not,' Torey said more breezily than she felt. The hairs on the back of her neck were still standing on end.

'Tell him that,' Gino said, directing her towards a shiny black Datsun 280Z. 'Your grandmother should get a sign in her yard that says, "Beware of attack tenant".'

Torey laughed. 'He's not that bad.'

'It wasn't your arm he was trying to break.' Gino disagreed.

He drove them to an authentic-looking Mexican restaurant on Pacific Coast Highway where he plied her with enchiladas and margueritas, telling her outrageous stories about what he had been doing for the past seven years, making her laugh until tears came to her eyes.

'Oh Gino,' she told him as he helped her into the car again and drove towards the pier in Redondo. 'I've needed this.'

'In love with me already, are you?' he grinned, brushing his lips across her hair before straightening up to ease the car away from the stoplight.

'Well,' she said, considering, 'it's not exactly love, Gino.'

'Not yet,' he amended.

Don't I wish, she thought. Would that it were that easy. He seemed to be everything she wanted in a man—kind, funny, intelligent, handsome, talented, loving. If ever there was a worthy successor to Paul, Gino was probably it. But that something special wasn't there. She didn't feel the same zing when his lips caressed her hair that she had with Paul. She didn't have the urge to snuggle up next to him and rest her head on his shoulder, toying with the blond hair at the nape of his neck. No, there was only one man now who incited those responses, one man who made her heart beat faster, one man who seemed able to melt the ice that had held her captive since Paul had died.

Oh Jake, go away, she begged silently. *Let me be.*

But Jake's was not an accommodating spirit. Where she and Gino went that evening, he went. Over the past two years she had got used to Paul's face intruding on her thoughts, but it wasn't Paul haunting her tonight. It was Jake.

'Have you had a good time?' Gino asked her as they stood on the broad pathway in front of Addie's house.

'Oh yes.' If only Jake hadn't come along in spirit it would have been fine.

'Then I can call you again?'

Jake's dark face flashed in front of her eyes. 'Yes, of course.' Her voice was more enthusiastic than it should have been, designed, she supposed to banish his devilish blue eyes from her mind. But maybe if she saw more of Gino, she could fall for him. It was worth a try. Proximity might do the trick. It seemed to work with Jake whether she wanted it to or not!

'Good.' Gino leaned over and gave her a quick kiss on the lips.

No melting, no conflagration. Not even a spark. Damn, Torey thought. But Gino didn't seem displeased, and Torey decided that even if she didn't hear violins or angels singing, at least she felt comfortable with Gino. Time, that was what she needed. Love hadn't been a whiz-bang affair with Paul either.

'Thanks for a lovely evening,' she whispered, grateful that Gino didn't press to come in.

She slipped off her shoes in the dark entryway, hoping that her tiptoed entrance wouldn't wake Gran. Smiling slightly, she sent a thank-you winging to Jake who, for all his faults, must have persuaded her grandmother to get some sleep. Thank heavens. She didn't need a grandmotherly inquisition tonight.

'Ten more minutes and you'd have turned into a pumpkin,' a voice drawled out of the living room's darkness.

Torey spun around to glare into the unlit room. 'What on earth are you doing here?'

'Meditating?' Jake offered, and Torey heard the creak of the rocking chair as he got to his feet.

'Why aren't you at home?' She moved to switch on the light, but Jake put out a hand and caught hers.

'Don't. It shines into Addie's room.' He led her into the kitchen where he released her hand, then shut the door and flicked on the tiny light over the stove. It gave just enough light for her to make out the ruffled dark hair that drifted across his forehead and the unbuttoned state of his shirt. 'Coffee?' he asked with disarming calmness.

'No! I want to know why you're still here! Were you spying on me? My God, even Addie didn't think she had to wait up and see me home.'

'Because I offered,' he countered logically. '*You* told me to get her to go to sleep. She wouldn't unless I waited up for you.'

Torey gnashed her teeth. 'That's absurd. If she was worried you could have just waited until she was asleep, then gone home.'

Jake shrugged. 'I didn't mind.' He was looking at her

as though she was the unreasonable one. 'Sure you wouldn't like some coffee?' He turned on the kettle and settled into one of the chairs.

'Help yourself,' Torey said. 'I'm going to bed.'

'Can't. Scott's in there.'

'Take him home then!'

'All in good time,' Jake soothed. 'Why don't you just sit down like a good girl and tell me all about Prince Charming?'

'Prince Charming is none of your business!'

'Where'd you go to eat?' he persisted.

'I said, "It's none of your business."'

'Not even where you ate?' Jake sounded wounded to the quick.

'A Mexican place on Pacific Coast Highway,' Torey spat out.

'I didn't know you liked Mexican food.'

'What you don't know about me would fill volumes,' Torey said, resisting the interest she saw in the cool, blue eyes and tapping her fingers nervously on the table.

'True,' Jake conceded. 'But I'm learning. *I want to learn, Torey.*' He leaned forward fixing her intently with his gaze.

'Why?' Torey asked hoarsely, staring at the clock over his right shoulder. It was the witching hour. The kettle whistled and Jake got up and made himself a cup of coffee with the concentration of a cordon bleu chef. Torey wondered if he hadn't heard the question.

'Because I'm attracted to you,' he said finally, turning back and watching her with hooded eyes. 'And you are afraid of me.'

'I am not.'

He looked sceptical. 'You've been running in the other direction since you got off that plane. Why? You used to want me.'

Torey hoped fervently that the light was dim enough to hide the colour flooding into her cheeks. 'That was years ago,' she stammered. 'I was a stupid, innocent child.'

'And now you're a big, brave woman,' Jake jeered. 'So why are you running away?'

'Did it ever occur to your conceited ego that I might have got two cents worth of sense over the past seven years? I met Paul and I found out what true love really is. And what it's not.' She slipped her plait back indignantly. 'And I have no intention of settling for less the second time around.'

'Take that,' Jake said with tightly controlled lightness which was belied by the whitened knuckles clutching his coffee mug.

'Enjoy your coffee,' Torey said frostily. 'I will carry Scott up to your place myself.' Turning on her heel she walked out of the kitchen. She was about to lift Scott's limp form from her bed when Jake shoved past her.

'Don't strain yourself,' he muttered and hoisting his son easily in his arm, he strode out of the room, an anger she didn't completely comprehend emanating from him.

Torey followed him through the kitchen, noting the jerkiness of his movements as he shouldered his way out the door. 'Can I help?' she offered.

'No.' His voice was rough. Then he growled, 'Pleasant dreams,' and kicked the door shut behind him.

Pleasant dreams ha, Torey thought as she slipped into bed a few moments later and felt the small warm spot where Scott had lain as though it were an ache deep inside her. Were there such things as pleasant dreams any more? She sighed, hugging her pillow and feeling a desperate loneliness she hadn't experienced since the first raw days of missing Paul. That had been real love, true love. But was it the only kind there was? Would she even recognise it if she found it again? And could she possibly find it the second time around?

CHAPTER SIX

SOUNDS of *Chopsticks* interspersed with *Peter, Peter, Pumpkin Eater* woke her. Torey yawned and stretched, letting the childish melody wash over her like the warmth of the late morning sun angling through her window and casting a white glare across Paul's picture. She smiled over at him as she did every morning, though she could barely see him because of the reflection. She lay back and tried to remember weekend mornings when he would get up to do the milking and she would make coffee, and then they would take the morning paper and cups of coffee and sneak back to bed. But not to read. She rubbed the cool sheet against her cheek, her eyes pressed shut, trying to recall the feel of him, the warmth. Her throat tightened and she swallowed hard, realising that the lips she was recalling were not Paul's, but Jake's hard and persuasive against her own.

Damn him! She flung back the covers and got up. *Peter, Peter* continued relentlessly in the living room. No wonder she couldn't rid herself of images of Jake—his son was in the house that very moment. Perhaps Jake was too. She hoped not.

Nevertheless, she took pains to do her hair up in a neat plait and then put on a sunny yellow terry jumpsuit that made her look far more confident and cheerful than she felt. She needed all the psychological advantages she could get when she faced Jake Brosnan. Finally giving in to the smell of coffee and bacon she squared her shoulders and left her room.

Scott had switched to *Heart and Soul* now, and Torey thought that if she didn't add to his repertoire soon, it was going to be a very long summer. He stopped when

81

she appeared and grinned. 'Good. You're up. Wanta go to the beach?'

'Hello to you, too,' she said lightly, looking around carefully as if Jake might pop out of the broom closet at any moment. But he was nowhere to be seen.

'Have some breakfast,' Addie suggested, nodding to the stove where a plate of bacon sat, still warm. 'Thought the smell of it might get you up. Scott's been waiting for you to go to the beach with him,' she added as Torey forked bacon on to her plate and popped bread in the toaster.

'Why doesn't Jake take him?'

'Jake's working,' Addie said complacently. 'Anyway, I'm sure you won't mind. I told him you wouldn't.'

I'll bet you did, Torey thought glumly. Probably arranged the whole thing. She wrinkled her nose in annoyance. But then she caught Scott's eye and saw his lower lip jut out in disappointment, just as though he knew what she was thinking. It wasn't fair to take his father's sins out on him. 'I don't mind,' she said, giving Scott a warm smile. 'We can go down right after I put in the laundry.'

'Great!' Scott's face lit up and he dashed back to the living room. 'I'll play the piano 'till you're ready.'

Peter, Peter began again with tremendous enthusiasm, and Torey finished her toast to its rousing accompaniment. The rhyme reverberated in her head, 'Had a wife and couldn't keep her'. Like Jake? she wondered. Why hadn't he been able to keep her, whoever she was? Surely a son like Scott would have been difficult to leave. Torey would have adored having a son like him. It was just Jake manipulating her into caring for Scott that she resented.

But then, she thought as she loaded the washing machine, maybe that's how Jake's wife felt too. Maybe he had gone off to 'work' and had left her all the time, too. What work was he doing? Painting and sketching for his dragon book? She doubted it. He liked solitude for that; and warm southern California weekends like this one brought people to the beaches in droves. No, more likely he was 'working' on his current relationship with some woman, enjoying himself without the encumbrance of his five-year-old son.

As much as she resented Jake's having thrust Scott on her (with Addie's blessing, she admitted grudgingly), she thoroughly enjoyed their day at the beach together. Scott was outgoing, introducing Torey to lots of people. She even found herself agreeing to meet one young man for a beer that evening, hoping that he might become a friend like Gino or even more, like Paul. Not, she thought, like Jake.

They returned to Addie's just past four and she persuaded Scott to rest for a while, annoyed to note that Jake still wasn't back. Taking a quick shower she joined Addie in the living room where her grandmother was sitting in her rocker and doing the *Times* crossword puzzle.

'What's a four-letter word for irritating,' Addie asked.

'Jake,' Torey supplied instantly, then flushed as Addie's eyes fastened on her with eagle-like perception. 'Well, I mean, why isn't he back yet? Does he think I have nothing better to do all day than take care of Scott so he can mess around?'

'Jake's not messing around,' Addie said in mildly reproving tones.

'I'll bet,' Torey muttered. She avoided Addie's gaze, then turned and hurried into the kitchen, returning with a duster. With great concentration she removed the acre of family portraits from the top of the piano and began to dust. 'You need to do your exercises, Gran,' she said, changing the subject.

'Tonight,' Addie promised. 'While you and Jake are . . .'

Torey spun around, hands on hips, her green eyes flashing fire. 'Gran, Jake and I are *not* doing anything tonight! I already have a date.'

'You let some stranger pick you up on the beach?' Addie sounded shocked.

'Scott knew him,' Torey said defensively, taking a savage swipe with the duster.

Addie looked unconvinced. 'I'll ask Jake about him,' she decided.

'You will not!' Torey knocked her parents' 25th anniversary photo on to the floor. She heard the screen door bang.

'What won't Addie do?' Jake asked, appearing in the doorway with two large boxes of fish and chips in his hands. His face was sunburned, his dark hair still damp from the shower, and his silvery blue eyes sparkling with interest and amusement. Almost overpowered by her attraction to him, Torey jerked back and went on with her dusting, saying,

'Never mind.'

'Torey has a new young man,' Addie began.

Jake frowned. 'Who?' His voice was a growl and he banged the boxes down on the coffee table and dragged it over in front of Addie's chair. 'Help yourself,' he said to her. Then, 'What young man?'

'Gran,' Torey began warningly.

'She met someone at the beach today and she says she's going out with him,' Addie explained. 'Do you think it's a good idea?'

'Hell no. What do you know about him?' he demanded, turning towards Torey, his eyes locking with hers.

Torey flicked the duster impatiently. 'For heaven's sake, I'm not your daughter! Scott introduced us. His name is Tony Bates.'

Jake rolled his eyes. 'And you think *I'm* a wolf?'

'He seemed perfectly nice.'

'Oh sure. He probably thinks you will be too,' Jake leered. There was no doubt what he meant by 'nice'. It brought back memories of their disastrous first date, and Torey felt her cheeks burn.

'Drop it,' she snapped. 'Just eat your fish and leave me alone.' She turned to go to her bedroom, but Jake caught her arm.

'Sit down and eat.' It was almost an order. Torey longed to snap back at him or jerk away, but she saw Addie watching them with undisguised interest and decided that sitting down and eating his damned fish was a more mature reaction than stomping off in a huff.

'Thank you,' she said with tightly controlled violence. 'I will.'

Apparently as willing as she was to let the matter drop, at least for the moment, Jake turned the topic to Addie's exercises and once Scott had emerged, there was no lack of conversational topics. He catalogued everything he and Torey had done that day and Torey found herself blushing again and avoiding Jake's clear gaze of approval. It's only that you're useful to him, she reminded herself, before she could read something more into it. And to defend herself further she looked at him over the chips box and said tartly,

'I suppose you had a hard day on the beach as well.'

'It's always hard when it's crowded,' he said, which surprised her. She thought he'd deny being there at all. Irritated, she finished her dinner in silence, letting Scott's chatter wash over her, not really hearing what was said, wishing her grandmother hadn't mentioned her date with Tony to Jake. When she got up to carry the boxes into the kitchen he followed her and shut the door behind them. 'What bar are you going to?' he asked once they were alone.

'What makes you think it's a bar?' she demanded, though it was.

'With Tony it always is. Listen, Torey,' his expression was one of earnestness, like a big brother trying to prevent his little sister from making a 'big mistake'. She wanted to smack him. 'Some of these bars—and these guys—are way out of your league.'

'Out of my league!' she spluttered. 'You hypocritical

prig! I am not some naïve little hayseed anymore! So just take your opinions and put them where they'll do you the most good!'

'It's not me who needs them doing him good,' Jake said evenly. 'It's you. But I might've known you'd be too damned stubborn to take any advice.' His light eyes were boring into her and she turned away, grabbing the boxes off the table.

'From you any advice is questionable,' she said coldly as she shredded the boxes into the bin, wishing they were Jake.

Jake sighed and shook his head. 'Suit yourself,' he muttered, then turned and walked out of the kitchen, letting the door bang shut behind him.

Damn him, oh damn him! Torey wiped angry tears from her eyes, glad he hadn't seen them. He treated her like she was seven years old and, she thought angrily, sometimes that's about how old he made her feel! Well, tonight she would show him! She had changed since she was seventeen. She might not have been able to handle wolves then, but she knew she could now! She crammed the lid on the bin and went back into the living room to find Jake listening to another of Scott's stories about their day.

'Wish I'd been there,' he said and ruffled his son's hair.

I'll bet, Torey thought and lifted her brows with a sceptical look that was designed to let Jake know he wasn't fooling her.

He just grinned unrepentantly. 'Lying on the beach all day, soaking up the rays. What a life!' he said with a teasing glint in his eyes.

'So much softer than yours,' she retorted sarcastically. 'Did you work very hard, Jake?' she asked with false sympathy, curling into the big chair next to the window.

'It was rough,' he said seriously, and rubbed a weary hand inside the collar of his navy blue polo shirt. Torey looked at him, startled, but then she decided that, despite his serious tones he must have heard her sarcasm and, unable to defend against it, had decided that the best response was none at all.

'What a pity,' she mocked. 'Since you're so tired you'll need an early night, won't you?'

Jake's eyebrows lifted, then drew together into a frown, but he didn't reply.

'Come and play catch, Dad?' Scott implored, tugging at his father's arm.

'All right.' Jake allowed himself to be pulled to his feet. Unwillingly Torey let her eyes travel up the long length of his body wishing that he weren't so damned attractive. He still wore a pair of blue jeans better than anyone she had ever seen. Even the muscular farm boys at home—even Paul—didn't have quite the same attractiveness that Jake did. She jerked her gaze away, concentrating instead on the bare toes in the thongs he wore. Damn, even his toes were sexy.

'Wanta come along, Torey?' he asked, reaching down to yank on her plait as though she were a child.

'Thank you, no. I'll just get cleaned up for my date.' She mustered all her poise and shaped it into a sweet smile which she bestowed on him through tightly clenched jaws.

Jake muttered something rude under his breath and raked a hand through his thick black hair disgustedly. 'I'll be back pretty quick,' he told Addie. Giving Torey a fiery glance that spoke volumes more than she cared to read into it, he banged out of the house and she heard his thongs slapping down the pavement as he followed Scott to the beach.

'You do try his patience, dear,' Addie said mildly, giving Torey a reproving glance before picking up the television guide and flipping through it to find out what was on.

'*I*? *I* try *his* patience?' Torey almost laughed. 'He—I—I have been taking care of his child all day while he's been out . . . out . . . Oh, who the hell cares where he's been! And now he comes home and acts like some stern father when he finds out I'm going out for beer with some man he probably hardly even knows!' She jumped up and crossed to the bay window, glaring out at his back disappearing down the street.

'Jake is a good judge of character, Victoria,' Addie said. 'You should listen to him.'

'And so whatever he says, I suppose?' Torey replied scathingly. Would Addie think she ought to go to bed with him if Jake thought it was a good idea? Or would Addie even believe that dear sainted Jake ever took a woman to his bed? Torey felt like clawing the curtains. Instead she gnawed her bottom lip until it nearly bled before she calmed down enough to say, 'I think I'll just take Maynard for a walk for an hour or so, before I go to meet Tony.'

'You'll be back before you go to meet this . . . this, um . . . this young man, won't you?' Addie asked, her disapproval evident.

'Yes,' Torey promised, putting a leash on Maynard and heading out the door, 'I just need to clear my head.'

Scour my mind. Scrub it clean. Rid it of all thoughts of Jake Brosnan. She walked along Ocean Drive until she was out of the immediate vicinity of where Jake and Scott would be playing ball on the beach, then she cut down to The Strand and walked south towards Hermosa Beach, the evening sun casting long shadows before her as she walked. The breeze ruffled her hair, making her think of Jake's fingers tugging on her plait, toying with the loose strands. Stop it, she told herself, and began purposefully to concentrate on the sight of joggers loping along the hard-packed sand near the water, the surfers silhouetted at the breaker line, and the bicyclists who whizzed along the bike path, deftly threading their way through skateboarders and roller skaters. How different from Galena it was. Another world. Even she was different. Free. More alive. As if the emotions she had kept in mothballs since Paul had died, were once more in use again. And it didn't take a genius to figure out who was responsible.

Torey shook her head in dismay and, glancing at her watch, turned and headed back into the evening sun. Shading her eyes she looked back along the beach towards the pier. Two figures were playing catch near the volleyball posts—one tiny and blond, the other tall with dark hair. As she watched Jake leapt with athletic ease and speared a wild throw, then hoisted Scott on to his shoulders and strode back up the beach towards The Strand. A knot of desire grew in Torey's stomach as she watched them disappear. Would they be at Addie's when she got back? Lord, help me bite my tongue if they are, she thought. Another confrontation with Jake tonight she did not need.

He wasn't there when she returned however. But Scott was in the kitchen making popcorn with Addie. Maybe Jake had a date, too, Torey thought with a mixture of scorn and jealousy. Maybe foisting Scott off on them all day wasn't enough, maybe he was going out at night, too! Well, if Gran wanted to be taken advantage of, that was her problem. 'Having fun?' she asked with forced gaiety as she passed through the kitchen on her way to change for her date.

'Lots,' Scott said, mouth full. 'Want some?'

'No thanks.' She went into her room and undid her hair, combing out her plait and leaving it cascading freely down her back, constrained only by a bright red hairband. Then she put on pristine white jeans bought specially for her California trip—imagine wearing them for ten minutes on the farm, she thought with a grin— and a red top with spaghetti straps under which, of course, she could not wear a bra. She smiled approvingly at her image in the mirror. No, she was definitely a hayseed no longer. She suspected Tony would approve. But she added gold hoop earrings for good measure, twitching her lips at the alluring woman who grinned back at her. Take that, Jake Brosnan!

'I'm off,' she called to Gran as she headed towards the front door.

Jake sprang out of the chair where he was sitting. 'We won't be late,' he added, following her and taking her arm as she went out the door.

'What on earth are you doing?' she demanded, stopping abruptly on the porch and jerking her arm away from him.

'Going out for a beer?' Jake said hopefully with a smile that should have melted her, and would have if she weren't furious at him.

'Not with me!'

Jake shrugged. 'All right.' He shoved his hands into the pockets of his jeans and hunched his shoulders so that he looked rejected and forlorn.

Torey gave a snort of disgust and stalked away out of the yard and up the hill, purposely not looking back. How dare he invite himself along like that? she fumed as she walked. She turned the corner on Manhattan Avenue and glimpsed Jake following. Damn! He was ambling slowly up the hill, stopping to stare in a shoestore window, then studying a display of scotch whisky with the care of a liquor inspector. She hurried on, dashing across the street against the light, hoping to reach the bar before Jake saw which one she entered.

Tony was already there, nursing a pitcher of beer at a tiny table across the crowded room. Relieved Torey wove her way to his table. 'Hi, gorgeous,' he greeted her, his beer-laden breath reaching her clear across the table. He grasped her hand and pulled her down across from him so that they were staring into one another's eyes and their knees touched. His hand skimmed up her arm almost touching her breast. A shiver of apprehension coursed through her. Above the chatter and clink of glasses and the wail of a jazz trumpeter, she heard Tony say, 'I've been thinking of you all day,' in a voice that would have put Hollywood's latest heart throb to shame. His basset hound eyes devoured her as though he hadn't eaten in days. Torey edged back and grasped the pitcher, pouring herself a glass and taking a quick gulp for fortification.

'This is good beer,' she mumbled, feeling as inadequate as she had seven years ago with Jake.

'Not bad,' Tony agreed. He winked. 'I've got better at home though. I make my own,' he added in a low whisper. 'We can go there after a while.' He gave her a warm, slow smile calculated to melt her. Unfortunately she felt more frozen than ever.

'Well, er, my grandmother ... I ...' It didn't take Jake now to tell her that this had been a bad idea. Tony obviously had expectations she had no intentions of fulfilling. She glanced around for the nearest exit and caught sight of Jake lounging against the bar. He held a beer to his lips, but he wasn't drinking, just staring at her from beneath hooded lids. He looked like a panther about to spring. She straightened up swiftly as Tony's foot slid up her calf. 'I—the ladies' room,' she stammered, pushing her chair back.'

'Hurry back,' Tony said in a throaty whisper that made her skin crawl.

Not a chance. She took as long as she possibly could in the cloakroom in the faint hope that he might give up waiting and pick up a more amenable girl. But when she finally squared her shoulders and ventured back out into the crush of the bar, determined to tell Tony that their whole date had been a mistake, he was still there. But he was no longer alone. He was deep in conversation with Jake!

'You've met Jake,' he said sourly when she got back to the table.

'Torey,' Jake acknowledged, hooking over a chair so she had to sit next to him. 'Enjoying yourself?' His eyes glinted mockingly in the light from the red glass lanterns.

'Enormously,' she lied, downing the rest of her beer as quickly as she dared. 'But I should be getting back. Gran might need me. You don't mind do you, Tony?' she added.

Tony smiled somewhat feebly, and Torey wondered what Jake had said to him. 'Sure you won't go dancing later?' he asked with the air of a man who already knows the answer.

'Not tonight, thanks.'

'Not any night,' Jake muttered ominously.

'Perhaps I'll see you again at the beach though,' Torey continued, giving Jake a harsh glare. 'I've really enjoyed this.' She stood up.

'Yeah, me too,' Tony said glumly. He was already eyeing the unattached females at the next table. 'See you around.'

Jake swallowed the rest of his beer and got up to follow her.

'Don't rush off, Jake' she said saccharinely. 'I'm sure I can find my way home.' She practically bolted out the door, taking a gasp of the passing car exhaust and thinking how much fresher it was than the atmosphere in the bar. It would have been heaven, she thought, if only Jake Brosnan were not right on her heels!

Happily, though, he didn't say a word, but shortened his stride to match hers, keeping pace while she fumed inwardly about what an idiot she had been. So much for not being a hayseed.

'All right. Go ahead. Say "I told you so",' she snapped finally when he showed no signs of speaking and she couldn't bear the smug silence any longer.

Jake grinned. 'I don't have to. You did it for me.'

'I could have handled him myself,' she went on doggedly, digging herself in an even deeper hole.

'Uh huh.' It didn't take a hearing aid to catch the scepticism in his voice.

Torey muttered under her breath, feeling as foolish and humiliated as she had the last time they had walked together on The Strand seven years ago. Why, every time she made an idiot of herself, was Jake Brosnan there to witness it? Damn it all anyway! It would be a whole lot easier if she didn't find him so cursedly attractive. As much so now as she did then.

But the similarity to their first walk back to Addie's house ended in the front garden. Then Jake had bid her a gruff goodnight and had strode away without once looking back. Tonight he followed her into the living room and flopped down on the couch, leaving Torey to hover in the doorway as if she were the one who didn't belong.

'Sit down,' he invited, patting the space next to him.

'No thanks.' There was no way she was going to spend the rest of the evening sitting next to Jake, even if Addie was there to intercede.

He shrugged as if it made little difference to him, and Torey gnashed her teeth as she walked into her bedroom. If he didn't care, why had he bothered to trail her like some hired bodyguard just an hour earlier? She flipped on the light and discovered Scott asleep on her bed again. Quickly shutting it off, she groped for her nightgown and then barricaded herself in the shower. It was the one place she could go in the house where she could get away from Jake or his family! But even there she couldn't get away from her thoughts of him, and when she finally dried off and put on her robe to go back out into the living room, she thought she still heard voices and wondered, Good grief, doesn't he ever go home? It was nearly ten. Addie should be in bed.

Cane in hand, Addie was just going. 'I left the TV on for you,' she said. 'You found Scott?'

'I certainly did.' Torey's voice was dry.

'Jake will pick him up later,' Addie said, hobbling towards her room.

'You just put him on the couch when you want to go to bed. Jake will come in and carry him home.'

'Where *is* Jake?'

'Oh, he went to pick up Lola. He never gets back until late. Don't wait up,' Addie counselled her.

Of course not, Torey fumed. Just babysit his kid while he's out with some girl! No wonder he objected to her going out tonight. He wanted her 'services' himself. 'Gran,' she mumbled in strangled tones, but Addie went on, 'Good night, dear. Sleep well.' She paused in the doorway to her room. 'You never said, Victoria. How was your date with that young man?' Something glinted in her eyes that made Torey suspicious.

'Ask Jake,' she said drily. 'He invited himself along.'

Addie stifled a smile. 'He's concerned about you.'

'Humph,' Torey snorted. But there was no point in arguing about Jake with Gran. He kept all his failings well hidden from her. 'Good night, Gran,' she said, leaning over and kissing her grandmother's papery soft cheek. How different it felt from the weathered roughness of Jake's.

Was Lola feeling the roughness of his whiskered jaw right now? she wondered later as she curled into the big overstuffed couch where Jake had sat at dinner. There was still a faint hint of his shaving lotion in the air, and Torey drew a deep breath. Damn it, what did she care if Lola had her hands all over him? She had no need of philandering playboys, men who couldn't even accept the responsibility of caring for their own children, who just palmed them off on other people instead.

She left Scott where he was, knowing there was no way she could sleep. Her anger at Jake grew as the night wore on. She fed it intentionally, allowing her imagination to run rampant, urging it on, picturing Jake in the worst terms possible, compromising Lola and every other female who was willing. When he got home, she vowed, he was going to hear exactly what she thought of him, starting with his irresponsibility towards Scott and carrying over into his blatant use of other people (namely her and Addie), and dwelling especially on his wanton interference in her own life! She shifted irritably on the couch. Over thirty years old and last upholstered when durability, not fashion, was the watchword, it looked and felt like steel wool and did nothing to improve her frame of mind. It was almost a relief when the 'phone rang.

Expecting Jake, she was surprised to hear instead a soft, hesitant female voice. 'Mrs Harrison?'

'No. This is her granddaughter. May I help you?'

'Does she have a tenant named Jake Brosnan still?' the woman asked.

Torey sat up straight and brushed her hair out of her face. 'Yes.' Another of his women? she wondered. God, he must draw them like flies!

'Oh.' There was a pause, as if the woman couldn't decide whether to go on. Then she said quickly, 'This is Christy Brosnan, his former wife. I've been trying to reach him.'

Torey felt as if the other shoe had just dropped. If there was ever a night that Jake's former wife would call up out of the blue, this had to have been it. 'He's not around tonight,' she said flatly.

'Well, I have to talk to him.' This Christy was sounding agitated. 'I've sent him four letters and they all came back unopened. I thought he might have moved.'

'No.' Would that he had!

'I can't understand it,' the woman went on. 'Why would he send them back? Is there something wrong with Scott?' There was a note of near panic in her voice now. Clearly she wasn't indifferent to her son.

'No, no,' Torey reassured her. 'Scott's just fine.' Jake, on the other hand, was getting worse by the minute! How could he be so cruel as to deny this woman access to her son, to return her letters as if he and Scott no longer existed on earth?

'I want to see him,' Christy said. 'I'll call Jake. Oh no, I can't. His number is unlisted. Do you have it?'

'No, I don't,' Torey said. 'I'm sorry.' If she had she would have dialled it for the woman herself!

'Tell him then,' Christy said, her voice wavering slightly. 'You'll tell him I called?'

'Absolutely.' When she was reading him the riot act tonight, she would be only too glad to add another page.

'Thanks. I'll be in touch.'

So that was Jake's ex-wife *That* was the determined career woman? Torey shook her head. Unbelievable. She had sounded so wistful and lost somehow. No wonder Jake had run roughshod over her. She didn't sound like she had the backbone of a jellyfish. Torey jumped off the couch and paced back and forth across the room, her fists clenching inside the pockets of her yellow robe. Too bad he didn't show his face right now, she thought. I've got enough back-bone for both of us! She growled and muttered and kicked at the floor pillows, wishing they were the rear end of a tall, dark haired devil she knew.

'He is,' she said to Maynard, 'the most insufferable bastard I have ever had the misfortune to meet.'

Maynard thumped his tail in agreement.

By two-thirty in the morning Torey had added more adjectives and several nouns to her description of Jake's character. It couldn't, she decided, sink much lower. Then she heard the truck pull up, the doors slam and, a few minutes later, instead of the door opening, the telephone rang.

'Torey?' he said when she answered, ready to let him have it.

'What do you want? Why aren't you over here? What'd you do, help close the bar?' she snapped at him for starters.

'Yes,' he said after a brief pause. 'Listen, keep Scott tonight, will you?' he went on in a rush. 'I've got Lola up here.'

Torey stared at the receiver as if it had sprouted wings. Keep Scott while he entertained some floozie all night? *All night?* He'd just hit rock bottom. Her fingers clenched around the receiver.

Jake seemed to take her silence for acquiescence, not stupefaction, for he went on hurriedly, 'Thanks a million. See you tomorrow.'

Torey stood transfixed for a full minute before she hung up. See you tomorrow? You'd better believe it, buster, she thought savagely, letting the pillow have another swift kick as she strode through the living room to the kitchen where she stared unblinking at the dim light in Jake's living room. I'll see you tomorrow at dawn with pistols, she thought grimly. The slender silhouette of a woman moved past the window. Jake followed. Torey gripped the edge of the sink, stiff with anger. Then the light in his apartment went out, and with it the pain centring in her chest grew. And grew.

The night lasted a lifetime. Maybe two. But shortly after seven, just when she was beginning to doze on the ironhard couch in the living room, she heard a door bang and she tore into the kitchen to see Jake and a pretty young blonde woman come down his stairs. Puzzled, Torey flung open the door, gathering her wits and her anger and descending the stairs to do battle. She hadn't imagined he'd be up for hours yet. But then maybe he had wanted to get rid of his bedmate before Scott woke up and went home. 'Jake!' she yelled as he was about to follow Lola into the garage.

He stopped and turned to look at her. She didn't doubt that she looked like a hag, hair dishevelled, robe askew, sleepless eyes red-rimmed with anger. But Jake didn't look much better. Too bad he'd had such a hard night, she thought savagely, taking in the dark shadows under his eyes, the nick on his chin from shaving, the uncombed hair. He was wearing red trunks and he had a towel slung around his neck. Surely he wasn't intending to jaunt off to the beach again! And who did he mean to stick Scott with now? 'What is it?' he asked impatiently.

'I want to talk to you,' she said. Scream at you. Yell at you.

'What about?' Jake looked pointedly at his watch.

'Last night. And Scott. And you taking advantage of . . .'

'Look, save it, will you?' he cut in. 'I've gotta get Lola home now or I'm going to be late for work.' Without giving her a chance to object he turned on his heel and stalked after Lola to the truck. Torey stood fuming, mouth open, in his wake.

Save it she did, with interest. She accepted Gino's invitation to go sailing that afternoon, leaving Scott with Addie. 'If you want to be taken advantage of, be my guest,' she told her grandmother. 'I am going out.' She wished she could have removed Jake from her mind as easily as she did herself from the premises. But all day long she wanted to have it out with him. To tell him off. For seven years resentment had been building, and tonight she was going to do something about it. If she'd entertained any doubts, they were banished the moment Gino brought her home and she found Addie exhausted and playing what might have been her fiftieth game of Snap with Scott. Torey felt fleetingly guilty and angry with herself for sticking her grandmother with him all day, but she immediately transferred that anger to Jake. Scott wasn't *her* son after all!

'Where's Jake?' she demanded when she came in the living room.

'I don't think he's home yet,' Addie said, but just then Torey heard his truck.

Scott jumped up, but Torey forestalled him. 'You wait here,' she commanded and stalked out to confront him at the foot of the stairs to his apartment.

'You been lying in wait all day?' he asked sarcastically, rubbing a hand through salt-stiffened, tousled black hair. He looked irritable and harassed, his face sunburnt except where the zinc oxide covered his nose and cheekbones. Like a savage, Torey thought, with warpaint. And let sling her first arrow.

'Where the hell have you been? Do you know how tired my grandmother is taking care of your son all day?'

Jake's jaw set in a hard line. 'Where were you?' he asked roughly.

'Out.' She hated it when he tried to put her on the defensive. 'I was out. I was not hired to watch your child!'

'No, you weren't,' Jake agreed wearily. 'And you'd never lift a damned finger to help anyone else, would you? Not even your own grandmother?'

'Me? So you could go out and play for two days? You must be out of your mind!'

'I was working, damn it!'

'Sure you were!'

Jake's eyes flashed fire, but he was silent, gritting his teeth in the face of her scorn. He turned abruptly towards Addie's house. 'If she's as tired as you say, I'll go get him right now.'

'Not just yet.' Torey grabbed his arm as he brushed past her and he spun around so they were scant inches apart. The heat from his sun-baked body warmed her and she stepped back instinctively. 'I have more to say.'

'Say it then,' he said tersely, his body taut with restrained anger.

'I don't want you ever again to leave Scott over night at my grandmother's while you entertain your women! What kind of father are you, anyway?'

'A lousy one, according to you,' Jake bit out, his fists clenching and unclenching at his sides.

'An irresponsible one at least,' Torey agreed. 'Don't you care what kind of an example you set for that boy? Why don't you give him to his mother?'

'Because she doesn't want him!' There was fury in his voice.

'Oh no?' Torey said scornfully. 'That's not what *she* told me!' She looked at him triumphantly.

Jake stared, thunderstruck, his face paling. 'You talked to Christy? When?'

'Last night, while you were out with your latest lady love. Is that why she left you, Jake?' she baited him. 'Too many women?'

'Damn you! What'd she want?' he demanded, gripping her arm.

'If you wanted to know, why didn't you answer her letters?' Torey jerked her arm away from him, rubbing it where his fingers had hurt. 'She says she sent you four!'

Jake shrugged, his eyes suddenly bleak. 'Maybe she did. Did she say she wanted Scott?' he asked, his voice threaded with anxiety.

'I don't know what she wanted,' Torey snapped irritably. 'She said she wanted to talk to you. About Scott among other things, I gather. She didn't sound surprised when I said you were out. Did you spend a lot of nights away from home when you were married, too?'

'Of course not!' He kicked the brick patio in disgust. 'And I wasn't out with Lola either! Hell,' he gave a snort of disgust, 'did you think I brought her home and called you up to babysit while I ravished her, for Christ's sake?'

'Well, I——' Yes, that was precisely what she had thought he was doing, though she might have described it differently.

Jake gave a bitter laugh. 'What the hell kind of opinion of me do you have anyway?'

'One based on experience!' There, she was on safe ground now.

Jake said a rude word. 'You are unreal! Just because seven lousy years ago I made a pass at you when I thought you wanted to go to bed with me, you have me pegged as the world's greatest villian!'

'Seven years ago, nothing! Last night——'

'Last night be damned! Everything you've been

accusing me of is a product of your one measly experience with me seven years ago! That and a fertile imagination. You never forgave me for that night, did you? Why? Did you wish I had taken you to bed? Were you frustrated because I didn't? And now, are you trying to make me out to be some sort of evil monster just because you were too young to know what you were doing then?'

'No! I never—I——'

'The hell you haven't! All I've heard from you is how you were so young and immature then, and how you've changed, how you've grown up! Well, what makes you think I haven't? What makes you think that I'm the same man you knew seven years ago? Don't you think I might have grown up a bit too?' He spun on his heel and strode away from her towards Addie's back door, his shoulders set rigidly in anger.

Torey closed her eyes and sank against the wall of the garage as she heard Addie's screen door slam viciously behind him.

CHAPTER SEVEN

IF Torey hadn't expected Jake to take her dressing down to heart and promise faithfully to reform, neither had she expected him to go on the attack. But there was certainly no other word to describe what had just occurred between them. Of course everything he said was patently false.

Wasn't it?

Torey shoved her hair back behind her ears wishing she'd had the sense to plait it so that it didn't blow about and asked herself angrily again, It was false, wasn't it? She chewed on her lip, wondering. What was it he had yelled?

'Everything you've accused me of is based on your one measly experience with me seven years ago!' Hardly. It was based on last night! And on all those previous days and nights when he had given her the come-on. Not to mention that summer when she was eighteen! She rocked backwards on her heels, deliberately remembering what had happened that summer. For years she had forced it out of her mind. Now, in the face of his fiery anger, she hesitantly decided to take another look.

Stuffing her hands into the pockets of her shorts, she turned away from the house and went out the back gate to the alley and walked slowly down the hill towards the beach, her eyes on her toes and the badly cracked pavement. She had rarely watched the pavement when she was eighteen. She had been too busy watching Jake. She had never felt about anyone the way she felt about him from the very first time she saw him. The attraction was instantaneous.

She had come down from her grandparents' house the

night of her arrival in California to enjoy her first walk along the shore. She had seen him then. He was standing with his back to her, his hands on his hips as he watched some surfers far out. Wearing nothing but khaki coloured swim trunks, he had looked like a bronze god, all muscle and sinew with a thatch of black hair ruffling the back of his neck. Her fingers curled into fists as she knew instinctively that she wanted to go up behind him and run her hands through his hair, then let them slide down over his shoulders and the ridge of his spine. Waves of heat had coursed through her as she stared. In eighteen years she had never felt anything like that before.

Or since, she thought with an honesty that startled her. Perplexed, she wrinkled her nose. Was that really true? Hadn't she felt such heat, such desire, for Paul? She stopped stock still on the edge of The Strand and considered this. She had loved Paul. She had felt warmth with him. Excitement. Passion. But flames? Spontaneous combustion?

No, she thought slowly. There had never been anything quite like that. She could see Jake now, in her mind's eye, as he had turned to see who had come up behind him. His light blue eyes were such a contrast to the rest of him that she was momentarily shocked, then even more attracted than ever. He had just looked at her, not speaking, his eyes saying more than her limited vocabulary could understand. They spoke of things that she, at eighteen was just beginning to comprehend.

She stepped off the pavement into the sand, cool now that the sun had gone lower to spread an orange glow in the sky. Walking towards the pier she stopped to watch a doubles volleyball game in progress. Did Jake still play? That summer long ago she had watched him for hours, loving the way his muscles stretched and bunched as he leapt for the ball and spiked it into the opposing court, and the way the sun glinted off his sweat-drenched torso and the sand clung to the dark hairs of his chest and legs. Face it, she thought, there's nothing you didn't like watching him do. In fact she kept her eyes on him all summer. She envied the women he dated, the board he surfed on, the food he ate. She kept a Pepsi can she knew he had drunk from until the day after their fateful date. It wasn't just his looks that fascinated her, it was the faint aura of wickedness about him. He seemed to attract women like a magnet did metal shavings. She heard him joke with Mick about his escapades, though when he knew she was eavesdropping he said nothing at all. The bits she heard though brought both pain and pleasure. She hated that there were other women in his life. But what he did with them only fuelled her imagination for what someday he might do with her. The fantasies she had that summer were like none she'd had before or since!

And finally there was the night Mick invited her along on their double date. She could hardly believe it. Talk about a dream-come-true! All day she had floated on a sea of nervous apprehension, dying to go, yet wondering if she dared, terrified of having to please J.B. But he had been pleasant during the concert, touching her back to guide her to her seat and slipping his arm around her shoulders on the way to the party. Exhilarated and tense, she had felt like a pressure cooker about to explode. The touch of his fingers made her shiver and, perhaps thinking she was cold, J.B. had drawn her more tightly against him. He liked her! She was sure he did! Perhaps he would take her out again, miss her when she went back east, write to her declaring his undying love! All the lovely possibilities had swum through her mind as they rode through the darkness to the party. And drowned shortly thereafter.

Mortified, humiliated, all her dreams crushed by his precipitate lovemaking and her inability to handle it, Torey had turned him for a hero into a villain in one short night. By daybreak she had exaggerated his wickedness all out of proportion. She wanted him to be at fault so she didn't need to recognise that she might have truly led him on, however inadvertantly, and that she might have been responsible for what happened because of the role she had cast him in all summer.

The J.B. she had created was a fiction—the product of girlish imaginings and desires, fleshed out in Jake's body and endowed with traits she had manufactured from overhearing snatches of conversation and gossip. She stopped and leaned against the cool roughness of a pier piling, looking back at Jake's apartment. How much resemblance was there, she wondered, between the man who lived there and the one she had created? And why, if she had been so foolish at eighteen, was she compounding that foolishness now?

Because, she thought, sinking down and wrapping her arms around her drawn-up knees, it made her feel more righteous that way. And more sure of her love for Paul.

Paul. Her chin dropped on to her knees and she stared at the sand and bits of broken shell beneath her feet. Everything she felt for Jake was so different than she had felt for Paul. Jake had been like summer lightning, slashing into her life, illuminating it for an instant. Then gone. And what was left was Paul.

Paul was a hearth fire. Steady, dependable, *there*. Just as he had been that summer when she had come home from California. Singed by lightning, she had taken a new look at the young man with the wide grin and engaging sense of humour she had known all her life. He salved her badly damaged ego without even realising it, making her feel desirable, attractive, womanly. All the things that J.B. had not. She and Paul grew into adults together, loving and laughing, and their marriage had been good. Torey knew she would have been satisfied with it for the rest of her life. But it was not to be.

And now, out of the blue, she was faced once more with Jake. To feel the same old attraction, the same foolish adolescent love she had felt years ago seemed absurd, almost like a repudiation for her love of Paul. And so, to defend it, and to protect herself from being hurt again, she had resurrected Jake's old image. She had turned him into a womanising ne'er-do-well, all evidence aside.

Hold on a minute, she told herself. What about Lola? What about Christy and the returned letters? Was that evidence or not? She wasn't sure. On examination she had to admit that it didn't seem likely he would have asked her to babysit while he 'ravished' that pretty young blonde. Scrupulous Jake who had hovered over her at the bar to defend her virtue from Tony hardly seemed likely to rush off and do some attacking of virtue on his own. In any case he seemed offended that she'd suggested it. She almost smiled recalling the look of outrage on his face. And Christy? Why had they got a divorce? There was no clear answer to that. Jake had never said. He had't talked about her much other than to say she wasn't a doting mother and wouldn't want Scott. So why would he refuse to answer her? Unless ... she groaned, unless he still loved her and was afraid to let her back into his life. A pain somewhere in the region of her heart made her turn away from that idea. But she couldn't erase it entirely. There was so much, too much, she didn't know. And Jake was so very angry. She couldn't actually even blame him.

But what could she do about it? Even acknowledging their mutual attraction, did she dare try to get to know him better? Did she dare let herself fall in love?

She lifted her head and watched as a surfer tried to ride a high rolling breaker. He teetered precariously seeming, any second, about to fall. Then, as Torey sucked in her breath, resigned to his disaster, he regained his balance and rode on. She let her breath out. He wobbled. Like me, she thought. If I dare.

There would be no smooth ride with Jake. He had been a source of turbulence in her life since she had met him. To pursue a relationship with him now if indeed he would even talk to her now—meant expecting the waves to be rough. If she sat back and let him pass her by, she wouldn't get hurt. But was that what she wanted? No, she decided. It was not.

The surfer fell, sucked under the white foam, his board skittering across the line of breakers towards the beach. As Torey watched, he bobbed to the surface and swam in, grabbing the board and turning back into the surf again. Shaking water from his eyes, he flung himself down on the board and paddled directly into the oncoming waves. An object lesson, Torey thought wryly, getting to her feet and dusting off her shorts. Not every ride is a success. But you never became a surfer sitting on the beach. And you never got to know Jake Brosnan if you pretended you didn't want to.

Smiling, she recalled Addie's words: 'There's a lot you don't know.' Too true, she thought as she headed towards the house. But I will know. I'm going to ask.

'A lifeguard? What do you mean, he's a lifeguard?' Torey almost shrieked in the face of Addie's complacent revelation. 'You said he was an illustrator!'

'He is. But he works part-time for the county as a lifeguard. A "recurrent" I think they call him. He's a very good swimmer,' Addie tacked on as though that explained everything.

'I know he is. I know a lot of good swimmers, but that doesn't mean they're lifeguards!' She couldn't fathom it. Even though she had come home and asked immediately, 'What was Jake working on today?' she wasn't prepared for the answer. She leapt out of the overstuffed chair and paced across the living room to stare unseeing out the bay window.

'Well, Jake is. A good one, too. He got some sort of commendation last year for a rescue.'

St Jake again. But this time Torey didn't reject that image out of hand. Before she had scorned anything good she had heard about him without stopping to consider whether she was justified. But now she remembered him, eyes blazing with fury as he shouted at her, his face almost as red as his trunks. Lifeguard trunks. She groaned. Damn, why hadn't she noticed? She cracked her knuckles in frustration. 'You mean he's been out there being a lifeguard all weekend?' she demanded.

'Yes. He usually gets calls on hot weekends and holidays. Whenever there are crowds at the beach.' Addie lifted her shoulders gently. 'I thought you knew that.'

'No.' Scott had babbled something about his dad working on the beach, but Jake painted on the beach, too. How was she supposed to know that this work was different? And she had accused him of playing all day! 'I'm sorry,' she said to Addie in a low voice. 'I shouldn't have gone sailing with Gino and left Scott with you. I should have stayed home or have taken him along.'

'Nonsense,' Addie said briskly. 'You didn't promise to watch Scott. I normally do it without a thought. It's a trade-off for Jake and me.'

'What do you mean?' Torey had a sinking feeling.

'Poor boy, I impose on him dreadfully. He does all my grocery shopping, sees that the bills are paid, walks Maynard, takes him to the vet, keeps my car running. When I was in the hospital, he came to see me every day. When something breaks, Jake fixes it or knows someone who can!' Addie smiled and Torey felt ill. So much for him taking advantage of *her*! 'Besides, I like watching Scott. We have fun,' Addie finished.

'I know, but I should have helped you today,' Torey wailed. 'You weren't ready for him for two full days!' Not to mention last night, she thought. Nothing Addie had said so far absolved him of that. She licked her lips and dared to ask, 'Who is this Lola?'

'Oh, did you meet Lola?' Addie asked, her face lighting with a smile. 'Such a pretty girl.'

Torey had registered that much. But that wasn't what she wanted to know. She wanted to know who Lola was, more specifically, *who* she was to Jake! 'Yes, she is. But who is she?'

"Well, as I understand it, she's from Jake's home town. He sort of "keeps an eye on her". At least that's what he told me. Why?' Torey thought she saw a twinkle in Addie's eye. 'Jealous?' her grandmother asked.

'No,' she retorted quickly. Then, recalling her new resolution for honesty where Jake was concerned, she amended that to, 'Curious mostly. I just wondered if she was his girlfriend.'

'Hard to say,' Addie replied, her eyes on the vegetables she was paring. 'But I don't really think so. That isn't to say that he hasn't dated her. I know he has. But mostly I think she's just a family friend. She works as a cocktail waitress and sometimes things can get a little too rough for her on a Saturday night, Jake says. So he goes to pick her up.'

Torey didn't know whether to be comforted by that revelation or not. Obviously Jake liked Lola and was concerned about her welfare. It made believing that he had taken her to his apartment and ravished her rather difficult, but it still didn't explain what she was doing there all night. For once, though, Torey didn't want to undermine Addie's opinion of Jake by asking her. 'Oh,' she said, because she couldn't think of anything else.

'Jake doesn't date much,' Addie volunteered, and Torey's ears pricked up. 'He spends all his time painting and doing things with Scott.'

'What happened to his wife?' Torey asked, feeling like she was about to step into a mine field.

'They got divorced when Scott was two. They were together when they first rented the apartment. But she wasn't around much even when they were married. She's a stewardess, and I believe she wanted a career, not a child. So Jake raised him. Eventually she left for good. That's when I got to know him a bit more.' Addie was staring off into space, her pan full of carrots forgotten as she recalled her early meetings with Jake and his former wife. Then, shaking her head sadly, she picked up the knife again and sighed, 'She was a fragile little thing. Kind of lost. Young and confused when I knew her. A lot like Jake was actually. They looked like they didn't know what hit them.'

Torey couldn't believe they were talking about the same Jake. She couldn't envision him confused or lost. He had always seemed so totally in control of every situation. Even the night she had so clumsily refused his lovemaking, he had only been disorientated a few seconds. Then he was in command again, cold and distant but controlled. 'I can't quite imagine that,' she began, and Addie interrupted,

'Of course you can't, my dear. You and Paul had something wonderful. Something to be envied. Even after Paul died and you were alone, I suspect Jake envied you.'

'What?'

'Your relationship was beautiful, positive. It was obvious in every picture you sent, pictures he saw. Even after it was over, you still had good memories. Jake doesn't even have that.'

'Surely he must have some,' Torey argued. 'He must have loved her when he married her.'

'I don't know,' Addie replied. 'He never said.'

Torey wished he had. How he felt or didn't feel about his wife nagged at her. But regardless of what he felt, he was a very different person in her mind that night than he had been in the morning. Her defences towards him had softened, melting away in the face of visions of him lost and confused, hurt by his broken marriage, struggling to provide for his son and caring for his elderly landlady.

Don't go overboard, she warned herself. You had him on a pedestal once before and look what happened.

But that time she had seen him as a romantic hero, the man of her dreams. Now she saw him as a flesh-and-blood person. A man with strengths and weaknesses, talents and blind spots. And she knew that she wanted to know that man. She only hoped Jake would give her a second chance.

After three days Torey knew that any chance she got would be of her own making. Jake was giving nothing away. He had apparently taken her words to heart for Scott was notable by his absence. Addie was bereft, Torey plagued with guilt.

'I'll apologise,' she promised Addie, explaining what she'd said. But apologising meant confronting him, and Jake was about as easy to confront as a cottontail rabbit. The most she saw of him was his thatch of black hair or the sight of his broad shoulders going in the opposite direction. Deciding finally to face him in his own apartment, she waited until after dinner one night when she knew the truck was in the garage and, heart in her throat, she mounted the steep stairs.

'Is, um, your dad home?' she asked Scott, scanning the room behind him but seeing only a thick, chocolate-coloured carpet, two leather armchairs and a sand-coloured sofa. No Jake.

'He's surfin',' Scott said. 'Wanta watch this show with me?' He nodded at the television which Torey saw flickering in the background.

'Addie's watching the same show,' she said, hoping it were true, 'and I made a cherry pie this afternoon. Why don't you come down?'

'Dad said to stay here.'

Guiltily, Torey nodded. She knew why. 'I'll tell him where you are,' she promised. 'I want to talk to him.' She waited while Scott shut off the television and saw him into Addie's before setting off for the beach.

Jake wasn't hard to spot. He was sitting astride his surfboard a bit apart from the others who had gathered

for an evening of wave riding. As she stood on The
Strand he caught a wave, coming to his feet
immediately and edging up towards to tip of the
board. The wave curled cleanly and Jake was in a
perfect position. If she had ever wondered what the
phrase 'poetry in motion' meant, she knew now. The
fluid joining of man and nature mesmerised her and
she stood unmoving until he had finished his ride and
turned to paddle out again. Then, realising she had
missed her chance to catch him, Torey began to run.
By the time she reached the water Jake was in
position to catch another wave, but instead he looked
shoreward, then turned and paddled out beyond the
breakers before sitting up and trailing his hands in
the water.

Obviously he had seen her and had decided to wait.
Dropping her towel on the sand, Torey ran into the
water, the shock of it hitting her like an icy January
morning. Now all she needed was for him to catch a
wave in past her. If he meant to avoid her, he could do
it without trying. But he didn't move, straddling the
board easily, his black hair clinging like a cap to his
skull as he watched her with hooded eyes.

A wave rose between them and Torey lost sight of
him as she dived beneath the bottle green water. Then,
as she cut through to the surface, she saw his bare toes
before her eyes. 'Hello.' She flicked wet hair out of her
face and squinted up at him, offering a tentative smile
that he didn't return. He stared at her stonily as she
bobbed in the water beside him. Since he clearly wasn't
going to respond, she plunged on, 'Scott's at Gran's
and . . .'

'I told him to stay——'

'I know,' she said quickly. 'He was. But I thought
that if it weren't for my big mouth, he'd have been at
Addie's. So I sent him down.'

Jake looked annoyed. 'You said——'

'I know what I said. I was wrong. I came to

apologise. I'm sorry.' She looked up at him guilelessly,
her heart in her eyes. 'I think maybe you were right.'

For a second Jake didn't move. Then a grin touched his
mouth. 'You mean you *did* want me to take you to bed?'

Torey's cheeks flamed. 'Not that,' she spluttered. 'I
mean, I think you were right about my basing my
opinion of you now on who you were, or who I thought
you were,' she amended, 'seven years ago.' She met his
eyes, trying to read his expression, but he wasn't giving
anything away. 'Anyway, I'm sorry,' she said again.

Jake frowned as though he didn't know what to say.
Maybe he was more offended than she knew. 'You
swam all the way out here to tell me that?' he asked
finally, his brow dark.

Torey nodded, then giving a little shrug, she turned
towards shore. What else, after all, could she say?

'Wait!' He leaned over and took two strokes, reaching
down to touch her shoulder. 'I—I apologise too.' He
gripped her shoulder tightly or she would have sunk
from astonishment. 'I had no business yelling at you.'

Torey offered him a smile. 'I think I'm glad you did,'
she confessed. 'If you hadn't, I might really have
convinced myself you were "the world's greatest
villain" after all.'

'Why?' Jake demanded. He drew her towards him,
then, balancing carefully, lifted her so she sat facing
him on the board. 'Why did you want to?' he repeated,
his eyes intent.

Torey looked down, unable to meet them staring
instead at the few inches of slick fibreglass between
them. But then her eyes strayed to his tanned, muscular
thighs plastered with wet dark hairs, and the faded blue
swim trunks that did little to hide his masculinity.
'Because of Paul,' she choked.

Jake stiffened. 'I can't be Paul,' he said, his voice
remote. Then he grasped her chin with his hand, lifting
it so that she was forced to look at him. 'You have to
let go, Torey,' he said softly. 'He's gone.'

'I know.' She closed her eyes, unwilling to face so starkly that the only features she could see in the flesh or in her mind now were Jake's. Besides, she wasn't the only one who had a past. 'What about Christy?' she wanted to know, her voice quavering slightly.

Jake's hand dropped. 'It's not the same,' he said.

Did you love her? she wanted to ask. Do you still? But their tentative gropings towards each other were too new, too fragile. It was enough that they were angry no longer. 'All right,' she said, but she knew he could still hear uncertainty in her voice. She trailed her hand in the water, avoiding his gaze.

'Shall we bury the past and start again?' he asked.

She looked at him then, and his eyebrow lifted speculatively. 'Can we?'

'Of course.' He made a mock bow, tipping the surfboard precariously. 'How do you do, Miss. Or is it Ms? My name is Jake Brosnan. I was just sitting here on my surfboard when, much to my surprise, who should swim by but the prettiest mermaid I've ever seen.' He grinned and offered her his hand.

Giggling, Torey took it and wondered if it was pure electricity shooting through her or if the fish really were nibbling her toes. 'I'm pleased to meet you, Mr Brosnan.' Then, beginning where she should have years ago, she asked, 'Where are you from?'

'Iowa. A little town north of Des Moines. My father runs the furniture store and funeral parlour there.'

'Really?' She hadn't ever imagined him as a small-town boy. 'Why didn't you stay?'

Jake snorted. 'Are you kidding? I'd have ended up painting signs for feed stores. If I was lucky my dad might've let me do the make-up on the people he embalmed!'

Torey giggled at his pained expression. His opportunities there sounded no more vast than hers had been in Galena. 'You'd rather do dragons?' she ventured.

'I'd rather be free to do dragons or windmills or whatever I want.'

'I know exactly what you mean.'

'You do?' Jake looked doubtful. A ground swell rose beneath the rocking the board and he leaned towards her to keep them from tipping over.

Torey caught her breath. 'Of course. That's why I'm here.'

'Swimming?' He was breathing faster, his eyes darkening as he looked at her.

'Not here, stupid. In California. Here I'm free to choose my own husband.'

Jake's brows shot up. 'Are you holding auditions?'

She trembled. 'Of course not! I'm not planning on remarrying at all—or at least not soon.'

'Oh.' His expression was shuttered, and Torey felt suddenly cold, as if he had shut her out on a snowy winter morning. She shivered. The board tipped.

'Don't rock the boat,' Jake whispered, his expression softening slightly. He edged closer so their knees touched. Then he reached for her, his large hands holding her gently and drawing her towards him. 'I don't want you to think I'm auditioning,' he rasped, 'but I want to kiss you badly. Now.' The last word was as urgent as any she had ever heard, and the moment he uttered it his lips came down on hers, parting them to delve within. Instinctively Torey wrapped her arms around him, clutching the sleek damp skin of his back, revelling in the heady mixture of salty air, lime shampoo and the indefinable essence of Jake that assailed her. They floated, rocked, tipped.

'Heads up!' The shout came from far off as the board lurched under the force of Jake's passion, and Torey raised her eyes to see a wall of green water rising behind him and heading their way.

'Jake!' She dragged her mouth away from his. 'Jake, look!'

Jake looked. 'Jesus. Lie down,' he ordered.

Torey did, flipping over on to her stomach, feeling Jake drop down flat on to her back, paddling madly to get in position before the wave broke over them.

'Dig in!' he shouted as the water surged around them, lifting and drawing them into the curl, then hurling them downward with mindblowing force. Torey paddled furiously, aware only of streaming cold water on either side and the heat of Jake's body on hers. There was no question of standing, of being clever, but Torey didn't care. She would rather ride this way, with Jake's chin on her shoulder, his mouth by her ear, his legs tangled intimately with hers.

'Some ride!' A teenager in baggy Hawaiian print trunks whooped as they came alongside him. 'Fantastic, huh, Jake?'

Jake stopped paddling, lifting his arms to let them tighten briefly around Torey before dangling them loosely in the eddying foam. 'Fantastic,' he murmured for her ears only, moving his hips against her so there was no doubt what he meant. Then, nipping her earlobe, he slid off, water streaming down his thighs as he stood, taking the board under one arm and slinging the other around her.

'Wave of the day, right?' the boy chortled, hopping around on the sand.

'Damn right,' Jake said and hugged Torey to his side.

CHAPTER EIGHT

She felt as if she were walking a tightrope—a giddy, precarious sensation compounded by the fact that Jake was inching his way towards her from the other end. Or, at least, she thought he was.

Outwardly nothing much changed during the next three days. Scott reappeared in her life, Addie's exercises went on without fail, Jake turned up for dinner and an evening swim. But the antagonism was gone, replaced by an almost electrical awareness charging the atmosphere between the two of them. Their eyes sought, probed, and slid away. Their fingers brushed, their voices caressed, and their silences spoke more than words would allow them to say. Was it possible that love was happening again? Torey wondered as she sat on the beach watching him swim, his body cutting through the waves like a shark. He caught a rolling breaker and rode it in to where Scott was jumping in the waves. Then lifting his head, he shook himself like a wet spaniel and ambled towards her, grinning.

'Come with me to the tidepools tomorrow.'

'Where?' She'd go to the moon if he asked.

'Palos Verdes. I've been sketching there this week. It's great dragon country. We can take Scott. All right?' He gave her a boyishly hopeful grin.

She nodded happily, and he beamed. 'Be ready by seven.'

Like a kid on Christmas morning, she was ready far before that, making a big lunch and then sitting like a kid waiting for the school bus, just inside the back door. Fortunately Jake was prompt. At seven she heard Scott's childish chirp in the yard, followed by Jake's peremptory knock on the back door. She straightened her T-shirt and shorts and opened the door.

'Ready?' He was leaning against the porch railing, a sleepy smile on his face that made her heart turn over.

'All set,' she said, proffering the wicker basket. 'I brought yogurt, salami, rolls and strawberries,' she explained.

'Good.' He took the basket in one hand and her arm with the other. 'We won't starve.'

She might, Torey thought, if the effect he was having on her appetite was anything to go by. She was much too busy feasting her eyes on him to bother with mundane things like food. Scott wanted to sit by the window again, so she found herself pressed against Jake, his thigh hard against her own, his shoulder brushing hers whenever he shifted gears.

'Sorry,' she mumbled as he brushed her for the fifth time. She tried to move over, but there was nowhere to go. Besides, she liked the feel of his arm.

'I'm not,' Jake said, slanting her a grin.

Torey suddenly felt about twenty degrees warmer. 'Jake?' she warned, but he only slipped his arm around her and squeezed her. 'Keep your eyes on the road.'

'It's not as easy as you think,' he grumbled. But as they wound their way up the tree-shaded road that led along the cliffs of the Palos Verdes peninsula, he had plenty to keep him occupied. And Torey, while she would rather have watched him, was persuaded by Scott to keep an eye out for whales.

'Have you ever seen a whale along here?' she asked after ages of futile searching.

'Nope,' Scott said, undeterred.

'Never,' Jake added. 'I've seen them up Santa Barbara way, but not here.' He slowed the truck and turned on to a narrow winding road that almost disappeared amidst eucalyptus trees and some low dense foliage that a midwestern Torey couldn't put a name to. They went slowly down the bumpy one lane road and halted near the edge of a cliff.

'Everybody out.' Jake hopped out and went around to the back of the truck, opening the hatch and removing the lunch basket and his case of art materials. Scott scrambled out too, and Torey brought up the rear looking sceptically over the edge to where the ocean roared beneath.

'Are you serious?' she asked, her heart clambering up into her throat.

Jake took her arm. 'Trust me.' His voice caused a shiver down her spine and she clutched at his shirt to save herself from slipping. 'I won't let anything happen,' he promised and she thought, that's what you think. There was plenty happening already and he was responsible for it all. But she took the basket when he handed it to her and let him slip his arm around her waist, holding her against him as he made his way carefully down the crumbling trail on the face of the cliff.

'Hey, look! C'mon!' Scott, part mountain goat obviously, was already skipping around on the rocks below, the waves lapping over his plimsolls as he pointed at something in a rocky pool.

'Hold your horses!' Jake called back as they skidded the final few feet to the narrow rocky beach. He set down the box and spread out the large blanket he took from inside it. 'There you are,' he said to Torey. 'All the comforts of home.' His eyes told her it was the bedroom he had in mind and she swallowed hard.

'Dad!'

Jake looked up helplessly, obviously torn between Torey and his son.

'Go on,' she urged. 'This day's for Scott, too.'

'Not *just* for him,' Jake protested, but he went and, after putting the lunch basket in the shade, Torey hopped down over the rocks to join them.

'Here.' Jake caught her hand and pulled her down

next to where he squatted on his haunches beside a tide pool. 'Stick your finger in here.'

Scott giggled. 'Oh, Dad!'

'Oh no, no you don't!' Torey protested, backing away after one look at the sea anemone Jake pointed at. 'Look, don't touch—that's my motto.'

'Not mine,' Jake said and slipped a cold wet hand around the nape of her neck.

'Jake!'

'You're scarin' the starfishes, Dad,' Scott complained. 'See the starfish, Torey?'

Shivering from the droplets of icy water coursing down beneath her shirt, Torey tried to pretend an interest in the starfish. All she really wanted to was to wrap her hands around Jake's neck. He laughed, jumping back out of reach and flicking more water at her as he retreated towards their blanket.

'Chicken,' she called after him.

He shook his head. 'No, just a hard working man.' He grinned at her, then bent to pick up his box of paints and sketching materials. 'Don't move,' he called to her over the sound of the waves. 'You look just like a dragon emerging from the sea.'

'Humph,' Torey snorted, pretending injury. She turned back to Scott, her heart beating with the fury of waves in a storm. Paul's teasing only made her laugh or smile. It never caused her to shiver with a fire and excitement all out of proportion to what was said. She knelt down next to Scott and feigned interest in the contents of the tidepool. But soon his enthusiasm was so contagious that she was really interested. There were a few species of marine life she could identify, more that she could not.

'We'll go to the library and look them up,' she promised. She nudged a hermit crab back into the pool and stood up, glancing over towards the blanket where Jake leaned against a rock, sketching something on the pad in his lap. His dark hair flopped across his forehead and his head was bent over the paper, then he looked up staring straight at her, and she grew warm under her gaze.

'C'mere,' he said, his voice soft and rough as he patted the blanket next to him.

Torey stared at him undecided, her gaze shifting from Jake to his son, still engrossed in the starfish, now prodding it with his finger.

'Come on,' Jake urged. 'He's fine by himself.'

Scott seemed oblivious. He was as caught up in marine biology as she was in a pair of marine blue eyes. Shrugging, she made her way across the slippery rocks to the narrow shelf of sand where Jake sat.

'Want to see a dragon?' Jake asked, a smile lurking in the corner of his mouth.

Torey gave a jerky, little self-conscious shrug, knowing the dragon would be herself. But when he tore off the sheet and handed it to her, she took it without thinking. It was nothing like she had imagined. A realistic—or idealistic, she thought—portrait, it was flattering in the extreme. There was no dragon in sight, just Torey with a wistful smile on her face, as if she were watching someone she loved without him being aware of it. Was this really how Jake saw her? she wondered, her throat tightening. Where was the shrew who had shrieked at him only days before or the starry-eyed teenager who had trailed after him worshipfully? This view was almost too good to be true.

'What?' she asked, her voice quivering. 'No fire and smoke? No scales and long green tails twitching?'

'Not on *my* dragon.' Jake took the picture gently from her hand, then caught her wrist and pulled her down on the blanket beside him.

'My—may I see the others?' she stammered, all too aware of the length of hair-roughened bare leg stretched out alongside her own.

Jake handed her the sketch pad, watching intently as she looked carefully through it. There were dragons everywhere. Pages and pages of them. Some breathing fire, some cuddling their young, some frolicking in the surf. She found herself smiling and wistful in turn, enchanted by the world of his sketchbook. There was one particular sad-eyed dragon who always seemed to be looking for something on page after page.

'Is this the one who's looking for his mother?' she asked.

'No. That's his father.' Jake's voice was so low she could scarcely hear him. He drizzled a handful of sand on his knee, then looked up for just a moment, favouring her with a wry, sad sort of smile rather like the one the dragon wore. 'He's lonely, too,' Jake added. His eyes were bluer than the ocean behind them, deeper too, Torey thought, drowning in them. A solitary seagull cawed nearby. Was Jake lonely? Did he miss Christy? Had he loved her so much that he had been devastated when she had left him? Torey wanted to ask, needed to, but couldn't. They had buried their pasts. Or were trying to.

'Which is the baby dragon then?' she wanted to know. And Jake pointed to one frolicking in the water, then on another page to the one nestled next to the dragon with the lost-looking eyes.

'Think he looks like Scott?' Jake asked. 'Scott wants him to.'

'There is something about the grin.'

'And the personality,' Jake added drily. 'Scott can be a dragon at times.'

'Oh?'

'Yeah. He's got this thing about mothers.' It was almost a reluctant admission. Jake didn't look at her, his eyes were fixed on the small boy crouching next to the tidepool, blond hair flopping in his face. Then he sighed and scratched his jaw. 'Maybe he does need a mother.'

Christy again. Did everything come back to her? Torey wondered. 'You aren't a lousy father, Jake,' she said guiltily, remembering her earlier accusation. 'Nor irresponsible. I know you care for him.'

Jake rubbed a hand over his face. 'I'm not saying it because of that. It's just a gut feeling I get at times, like there's not enough of me.'

'You do spend time with him,' Torey tried to reassure him. 'More than a lot of fathers do.'

'Of course,' he said roughly. 'I have to. I'm his mother *and* father at this point. But between the illustrating and the lifeguarding, I don't have all the time I'd like.'

'You have Addie,' Torey said. She wanted to add, And me. But she knew he didn't have her. Maybe it wasn't even *her* he wanted.

'Yeah.' He rolled over on to his stomach and rested his head on his folded arms. 'But I won't have Addie forever. Her being in the hospital made me realise that.' He shut his eyes and Torey would have thought he was asleep but his jaw was tense. Then he sighed. 'Sometimes I think he ought to have two parents, even though he scarcely knows what it was like to have them, he might be missing out.' One blue eye opened momentarily and looked at her, but Torey turned her head because she wanted to see love in it and she feared that she would not.

'I think I'll paddle,' she said, her feelings knotted like a ball of knitting that's been played with by a cat. 'Want to come?' she asked, hoping he would not. She needed some space, some room to put what he was saying in perspective. Was he sounding her out on marriage? Was he voicing his loneliness without Christy? Was there a place for her in the life he led?

She picked her way down the narrow beach towards a rock outcropping, then clambered up until she perched on a narrow promontory that jutted out into the surf. Looking back she saw Scott, still exploring the tidepools, and a wave of maternal feeling welled in her breast. She loved that child almost as much as she loved his father. But he belonged to Jake. And Jake? Who did he belong to? She shut her eyes and wished with all her heart that she knew.

'You won't get much paddling done up here,' a voice behind her chided, and Torey turned to squint up at him, noting the sunlit halo around his dark head.

'I have a strong imagination,' she grinned. 'And it's safe.' But not much, she reflected, remembering how much anguish she had provided for herself by imagining things in the past. Could she keep it in check now?

'Maybe,' Jake said. 'But I promised Scott we'd do it for real.' He held out his hand to her and, taking his rough, charcoal-smudged palm in hers, she allowed him to pull her up. They scrambled back over the rocks to where Scott waited, then took his hands between them and swung him high over the incoming breakers. Scott shrieked, kicking his feet, splattering Torey in the face.

'Devil!' she yelled. 'I'll get you,' and deliberately lowered her arm so that Scott got drenched.

'Come on, Dad! Let's get her!' Scott hollered, letting go of her traiterous hand.

He wouldn't, Torey thought. But the mischief sparkled in Jake's eyes and he leapt for her, joining his son in pursuit. 'Jake!' she protested, half-laughing as she scrambled away, floundering on the seaweed-slick rocks. She slipped and skidded into a tidepool, landing hard on her seat, and Jake dropped down beside her, catching her in his arms.

'Gotcha!' he grinned, kissing her hard on the cheek. Then tenderly he brushed damp strands of hair out of her face. 'Are you okay?'

'Wonderful,' Torey said, and reached around, grabbing his shoulders and shoving him underwater, then draped a strand of seaweed round his strong, tanned neck. He jerked his head up, spitting water, still laughing.

'Wicked woman!' He scrambled to his feet, offering her a hand up which she ignored.

'I'm soaked,' she moaned, glowering at Scott so that he giggled and danced away from her.

'I know the solution to that.' Jake's eyes travelled slowly down her entire body, detouring at every curve, sightseeing along the way.

'What's that?' She wrung out her hair, thanking God the water was cold, otherwise she'd have burst into flames beneath his gaze.

'Take everything off.'

'Don't you wish?' she growled, her throat dry. But at the rate he was going she wouldn't need to, the heat from his stare was drying her off.

'I do indeed.' And without warning he bent forward and kissed her soundly on the lips.

'Jake!' she jumped back, glancing at Scott. But Scott looked anything but disapproving. He looked like he'd masterminded the whole scene. Jake put his arm around her and led her unprotesting to the blanket, pulling her down on it and lying down next to her to share the warmth.

'Don'tcha want to play some more?' Scott asked plaintively, following them.

'Not now,' Jake told him. 'We old folks need a rest.'

'A rest?' Torey lifted her eyebrows. How did he think they were going to *rest* lying just inches apart?

Jake grinned unabashed. 'Well, *I* could use more than a rest,' he said, easing himself even closer so his thigh brushed hers. 'But I think, with the resident chaperon at hand, that may be all I have a right to expect.' His look was so surprisingly boyish and rueful that she couldn't help smiling back. As she did so, Jake lifted up on one elbow and turned to face her, reaching out to trace the curve of her lips with one long, sensual finger. Almost under their own volition, her lips parted and her tongue followed the path of his finger. Jake caught his breath. His hand lingered for a moment, rough against the softness of her cheek, then travelled down her neck to her shoulder, then continued lower to stroke the tops of her breasts through the wet T-shirt. His fingers were unsteady, and Torey watched them, mesmerised, powerless to stop them, not even wanting to. Then he bent his head, nuzzling where his fingers had stroked, his dark soft hair tickling her chin. She trembled. Jake's hand crep down and slid under her shirt, lifting the wet, clinging fabric and slipping across the soft skin of her midriff to tease the underside of her breasts.

'Take it off,' he whispered urgently, his mouth against her shirt, nibbling her through the cloth, causing her to shiver in delight.

'Jake,' she tried to protest. 'Scott——' She grabbed his questing hand, but he shook her off, making a wry face.

'The joys of fatherhood,' he muttered, but they weren't slowing him down much. 'You don't really need that bra, do you?' he asked huskily.

How was she supposed to answer that? Wet, clingy thing, of course she didn't need it! She only needed Jake's hands, fingers, mouth. A sigh, almost a moan, escaped her before she could stop it. Jake smiled, her fingers undoing the clasp with a sureness that bespoke experience. Shielding her body with his, he drew up her shirt, slipped off her bra and pulled the shirt back down, his hands settling beneath it possessively after he pulled it into place. 'There, that's better,' he murmured and his skilful fingers roamed and teased until she strained against him.

'Jake.' She breathed his name, heat coursing through her veins, raising her body temperature to new heights. Her hands moved to touch him, to feel the rough dark hairs drying on his chest, trailing her fingers over each rib in turn, then stroking his firm stomach so the muscles tautened under her touch.

Jake swallowed hard, barely breathing under her gentle caresses, and Torey smiled, heady at the power she felt. God, she had wanted to touch him for years!

All her earliest longings came back with the force of an express train, the pent-up desire contained so long. Her fingers brushed along the waistband of his cut-off jeans.

'Torey!' It wasn't a warning so much as a plea. His hands on her breasts stilled, hovering, waiting, his eyes glazed now with a desire she had never dared to imagine. Again her hand brushed him, touching the warm flesh of his stomach, the cool rough denim of the jeans. They stopped, lingering at the fastener, toying with it, wanting to pop it open, needing to, but scarcely daring.

Suddenly his arms wrapped around her, dragging her up hard against him. Her T-shirt pressed into his hard chest, her breasts flattening. His thighs strained against hers, hard and wanting. Jake's hands roamed across her back, weaving a spell with their seductive touch, causing her to mould her body closer to his. Waves roared. Or was it the blood in her ears? She didn't know. Her fingers slipped beneath his waistband, following the trail of dark hair. Jake's breathing grew harsh in her ears and his fingers slid inside her shorts, pressing her against his hips.

'Hey!' Scott called. 'Wanta see a jelly fish?'

Torey froze. Jake stopped breathing altogether. Then, slowly, she withdrew her hand, Jake breathed again, and they eased apart, eyes touching now, nothing else.

'If they sting, do they hurt?' Scott was asking, his voice carrying across the tidepool to the shelf of sand where they lay.

'No more than I do right now,' Jake mumbled, his eyes rueful as he shifted around to ease his discomfort. Torey smiled at him, then leaned across and kissed him on the tip of the nose.

'I'll go admire the jelly fish. You take all the time you need.'

'You're all heart,' Jake grumbled.

'Not all,' Torey teased him, happiness filling her soul.

'No.' He squinted up at her, assessing her. 'That's true. You have other attributes as well.'

'Which we won't mention,' she said, 'or you'll need even more time than you do right now. And Scott won't wait forever.'

'I know. I know. Another reason for having two parents, I guess.' Jake grinned. 'A mother to distract him while his father gets decent.'

Torey felt her face flush, and wished that he hadn't brought her up in the context of family. It was entirely too tempting to think that way. She turned and made her way down the rocks to where Scott waited.

'See 'im?' Scott pointed proudly to the diaphanous blob lolling in the surf just offshore. 'Isn't he great?'

'Terrific,' Torey agreed. The sun glinted off the water, setting the jellyfish in a diamond display.

'Think Dad would paint him?' Scott asked.

'I don't know.' Torey glanced back at Jake who was walking away from them, hands stuffed in the pockets of his damp, clinging cut-offs. She tore her eyes away. 'When he comes back you can ask him.'

But when he came back, Jake said he thought dragons were more his style, mother dragons especially, and slipped his arms around Torey, drawing her back against him and breathing fire down her neck. All the thoughts of Jake and Scott as family that she had been trying to banish came back at the speed of light, and Torey thought she was growing more than fond of sad-eyed dragons, too.

The rest of the day did nothing to lay those feelings to rest. Jake smiled at her constantly, his eyes saying things she could barely hope she was interpreting correctly. His fingers crept out to touch her whenever he thought it safe. While she was listening to Scott tell her about his teacher's trip to Mexico, Jake was sliding his fingers along her spine, tapping her back where her bra should have been and whispering, 'Thanks for the souvenir,' so that she blushed hotly and lost the thread of Scott's story. And almost didn't care. It was enough to have his father looking at her that way. It was enough to feel desirable to someone whose desire she wanted for a change. She had been guarded and unfeeling so long, that it was almost a miracle to love again. To share the feelings with Jake of all people was almost too good to be true. She watched as he tipped his head back and tossed a strawberry into the air, catching it in his mouth. Then he looked across at her and winked.

'Show me how, Daddy,' Scott begged, but Jake shook his head, smiling and getting to his feet, brushing the sand off his jeans.

'Not today. We have to get home. Torey will be a lobster tomorrow if we don't. We'll hear her howling clear over at our place,' he teased.

Scott looked at her amazed. 'Really?'

Jake nodded, face straight. 'And of course I'll have to go over and comfort her. Rub lotion on her back and . . .'

'You're forgetting Addie,' Torey interrupted, the red in her cheeks not only sunburn.

He grimaced. 'God, a grandmother and a son! Who's on our side?' he grumbled. 'Oh well, our time will come,' he promised with a leer.

And Torey followed him up the cliff with hope dancing in her heart. Their time—hers and Jake's! When? she wondered. Tonight? Tomorrow? Next week? It didn't matter when, she thought happily, it was enough to know that it would come.

'I'll just grab a quick shower then,' Jake was saying as he heaved the wicker basket on to Addie's back porch. 'Give me twenty minutes, okay? Then we'll go out to dinner.'

'Sounds great.' She felt grimy, ripe for a shower. But there was rapture where her mind should have been.

The back door creaked open and Addie appeared.

'Though I heard you,' she said with none of her usual smiles. Torey's sunburnt nose wrinkled at the sight of her grandmother's ramrod posture. 'You have a visitor, Jake,' she continued.

'Huh?'

A petite blonde woman appeared in the doorway behind Addie. Torey's mouth dropped open in recognition. 'You're——' she began.

'Christy,' Jake said heavily, his voice falling like lead into the silence left by Torey's astonishment. 'What the hell do you want now?'

CHAPTER NINE

'You look well, Jake,' Christy said in a soft voice as she came around Addie to look down at him.

Jake looked, Torey thought, sicker by the minute. The day's sunburn seemed almost to drain out of his face leaving him in grim-faced pallor as he stared back at her. He glanced quickly at Scott who was just disappearing up the steps to their apartment. 'What do you want?' he repeated, scowling.

'I came to see you. And Scott,' Christy said. Torey heard her voice waver as if she were expecting just the sort of hostile reaction she was getting.

'Why?' That one word contained so much negative emotion that even Torey stepped back, startled.

Christy shrugged slightly as she contemplated the apparent hopelessness of getting Jake to respond civilly. 'To tell you I'm getting married again,' she offered, as though it might help to make their peace. Torey sucked in her breath sharply.

Jake looked stunned. Then he snarled, 'Lucky you. Did you want my blessing? If so, you've got it. Better luck this time.' Then he spun on his heel and stalked off towards his apartment, taking the stairs two at a time, never once looking back. The door slammed hard behind him.

Christy was studying her sandalled feet in dismay. 'I was afraid of that,' she said. Pushing a wisp of white-blonde hair out of her eyes she sighed and turned to Addie. 'Thank you for putting up with me while I waited, Mrs Harrison,' she said softly. 'I don't know if you should tell him or not, but I will be back.' Torey saw a stubbornness in Christy's chin that made her feel a respect for the young woman she didn't want to feel.

131

Christy looked over and caught Torey's eye, considering her curiously as though wondering who her ex-husband was hanging around with now. But her gaze wasn't hostile, only interested, and then, on longer inspection, a bit perplexed.

'Haven't we met?' she asked Torey finally.

'Yes, once or twice,' Torey admitted. 'When I was visiting my grandparents a number of years ago. You were dating someone else at the time.' Christy had been. Mick. But Torey didn't want to mention that, fearing the memories it would bring, recalling how Jake had reacted to her mention of his friend. Besides, she didn't want Addie to know she had known Jake years ago, had dated him once. On a double date with Mick and the girl who was now Jake's ex-wife!

Christy's eyes brightened momentarily, then clouded with sadness. 'Yes,' she said, a hoarseness in her voice that told Torey how harsh the memories were. 'I remember now. You knew Mick?' The question was gentle, tinged with a kind of wistfulness that made Torey think of how she had sometimes sounded when she met and talked with some of Paul's old friends.

'Not too well,' she replied. 'He seemed very nice.'

'He was.' Christy's voice rose as though she would have continued, but then she seemed to think better of it for she shut her mouth, pressing it into a grim line. 'If you talk to Jake tonight, Mrs Harrison,' she said abruptly, 'tell him I'll be around. Tell him I want to see Scott.' She patted Addie's arm and walked briskly down the steps, the smile on her face stiff and unyielding as she crossed the yard and shut the gate.

'Oh my,' Torey breathed, leaning against the railing watching her leave, watching the warmth of her day leave too. 'When did she arrive?'

'About two hours ago. When she didn't find Jake home, she stopped to see me. We had tea and cookies and talked.'

'She's lucky she found you,' Torey said. 'I doubt she'd have got tea and cookies from Jake.'

'I think you're right about that.' Addie turned and went back into the kitchen, leaving Torey to follow. 'I'd no idea he was still so bitter.'

Neither had Torey. It depressed her at the same time that it lent creedence to her speculations that he still loved Christy. If he didn't why would he care if she got married again? Imagine Christy being his ex-wife! All the while she undressed for her shower she marvelled at it. Had he been harbouring secret longings for her all the time she dated his best friend? Torey ducked her head under the cool spray, scrubbing the sand and salt from her hair, wondering if seven years ago Jake had been longing for Christy while she, Torey, was longing for Jake! And when he got her it hadn't worked. There was a moral there somewhere, Torey thought dismally, whether she wanted to see it or not. Soapy water streamed down over her face and breasts, and she remembered Jake touching them and teasing them only a couple of hours before. Then they had tingled, aroused by her awareness of him. Now all her awareness was in the pit of her stomach which knotted as she wondered if, knowing that Christy was about to remarry, Jake would try to win her back.

It didn't seem likely, Torey had to admit, when he arrived freshly shaved and scrubbed an hour later. He made every effort to be genial and charming, teasing Addie about her first date out since her hospitalisation, giving Scott a ride on his shoulders from the parking lot to the restaurant, and calling Torey 'my favourite dragon' until she threatened to incinerate him with one breath if he said it again. But though Jake smiled and teased, there was a hollowness in his voice she hadn't heard before. His smile was forced, the teasing a bit too strong. He nearly shredded his napkin while they waited for dinner, and Torey longed to reach out and touch him, take his hand in hers, comforting him and promising him that everything would be all right.

But of course that was patently impossible. She didn't know for sure what, in his eyes, 'all right' meant. Jealously she didn't want to believe that it might mean that Christy would come back to him, and realistically she wasn't willing to tell him that 'all right' meant that she cared about him, would always be there for him, loving him and making his life complete. So instead she sat on her hands, trying to say with her eyes what she felt in her heart and wishing that Jake had good memories like she had of Paul, and that his memories, like hers, would recede into the past, letting them get on with life now. Jake, unfortunately, wasn't looking.

It was until they had taken Addie home and Jake was about to take Scott up to bed that he said to Torey, 'Want to come up and see my etchings?' He wasn't smiling, his face was dead serious, but she knew it wasn't etchings he was offering tonight. Nor sex either. It was simply that some nights, confronted by memories, it was better not to be alone.

'All right.'

He showed her where the coffee was, handed her a stack of picture books he had illustrated, saying, 'Behold the etchings,' and nodded towards the sofa. 'Make yourself comfortable. I won't be long.'

Torey made coffee, then curled into the corner of the sofa, adjusting a navy blue enamelled desk lamp over her shoulder for the best light. She was just beginning to look through his second book when Jake appeared in the doorway to Scott's room, looking sheepish, a dull red flush on his cheekbones.

'Do you tell bedtime stories?' he asked uncomfortably.

'One or two.'

'Could you?' An eyebrow lifted in entreaty. 'Scott wants you, not me.' It didn't seem to be an admission he liked making.

'Tell me a mother dragon story,' Scott demanded from his narrow bed.

Jake looked embarrassed, but moved out of her way
as she sat on the edge of Scott's bed. 'A short one,' she
agreed. 'The coffee's ready,' she told Jake. 'Go pour it.
I'll be out in a few minutes.' He wasn't the only one
feeling uncomfortable. She didn't need to feel any more
like a member of the family tonight, not when she knew
how much Scott longed for a mother and that his real
one had just appeared today.

Obviously Jake hadn't told him or there would have
been a million questions on his lips. She wondered why
Christy hadn't insisted on going up to Jake's after he
had left. But then, recalling the look on Jake's face,
perhaps it wasn't so odd. She wasn't sure she'd have
dared knock either. Not if, in time, she could come to
terms with him another way.

She told Scott a story about a mother dragon looking
for a child to love. She hadn't planned it, it just came
out that way. And while she felt almost tearful at the
end, Scott sighed and smiled contentedly, letting her
shut out the light and rejoin Jake in the living room
without protest.

'I think he's obsessed,' Jake said irritably when she
emerged. 'He's got dragons on the brain.'

'Mothers actually,' Torey corrected gently, going to
sit at the opposite end of the couch, needing the
space if she were going to be the least bit objective
tonight.

Jake sighed heavily. 'Yes, damn it.' His eyes closed
and she saw his jaw tighten. Then he muttered, 'What
the hell did she have to show up for?' He shook his
head wearily. 'Well, if I know Christy, she'd be gone
again tomorrow.'

Torey thought she detected a hopeful note in his
voice which pleased her because it made her think he
didn't care about Christy after all. But she knew she
had to disabuse him of the notion that he was rid of her
whether it pleased either of them or not. 'She said she
would be back,' she told him.

The blue eyes flew open, steely and cold, and Jake stared at her. 'She said that?'

'Yes.' Torey wished she had kept her mouth shut. She picked up her cup from the rattan and glass coffee table and blew on it gently.

'Damn.' Jake jumped to his feet and paced across the room, staring out the kitchen window into the sunset beyond the pier. But Torey didn't think he was paying the least attention to the picture postcard setting. His shoulders were thrown back, his hand stuffed into the back pockets of pale blue corduroy jeans. His posture spoke more of tension than of anything else, and Torey contemplated the wisdom of getting up and going to him, trying to massage the tautness from those muscles and ease the tension in his shoulders and back. It was what she would have done for Paul. It had never occurred to her to do it for anyone else. But she desperately wanted to do it for Jake now. She set down her cup and got slowly to her feet, padding across the thick carpet until she stood noiselessly behind his right shoulder. In the reflection of the glass she saw the tension in his face.

Jake took one hand out of his pocket and rubbed it around the collar of his navy and green striped polo shirt, easing it away from his neck in a gesture she had come to recognise as indicating his discomfort and anxiety. Then his hand drifted forward to rub absently at the scar over his eye. 'Sorry,' he mumbled. 'I guess I'm not exactly in the right frame of mind to show you my etchings now.' His self-mocking grin barely reached the corners of his mouth, but Torey felt it tug at her heart.

'Is there anything I can do?' Her hands went up behind him, beginning to knead his shoulders and neck. Her thumbs rubbed up and down on the cords of his neck, and he dropped his head forward, bracing himself against the window with his hands, encouraging her fingers to tangle in the thick hair at the nape of his neck.

'Shoot Christy?' he suggested with a hollow laugh. 'No. Just do what you're doing. God, that feels wonderful.' He sighed softly as Torey worked magic with her fingers across his shoulders, on his neck, and slowly down the ridged column of his spine. She wished she could ease his mind the same way. 'God, Torey, where'd you learn this?' He was shivering under her gentle ministrations, and Torey stopped the massage long enough to take him by the hand and lead him to the couch.

'I'm a physiotherapist, remember?' she reminded him, smiling. 'It's all part of the job. Lie down.'

He lay, obedient, on his stomach, his face turned to watch as she knelt next to him, his black hair drifting across his forehead shading the arctic blue of his eyes. She began to massage again, kneading the muscles near his shoulder blades, then sliding upward to work again on his neck before edging slowly and deliberately down the length of his spine. Jake stretched and arched his back, small almost primitive sounds catching in his throat as she moved her fingers along his spine. Reaching the waistband of his jeans, she began a languorous upward trek again, pleased to feel his tension easing. His eyelids flickered shut, then open again.

'You're a miracle worker,' he muttered, his voice sleepy.

Good, Torey thought. Maybe I can put you to sleep. She was grateful for his somnolent inclinations. They would be easier to deal with than his desire tonight. Together they had come a long way today. Far enough, she thought. It wasn't that many days since he had been a villain in her eyes. In the last week she had dared to give him a chance, dared to accept her attraction to him. But too much too soon would be as bad for them both as never knowing or trusting him at all. If she tried, she might even find it in her heart to be grateful to Christy for happening on the scene just now. But she wasn't quite that magnanimous. Not yet. Christy might still be a threat. Things between Torey and Jake were too tenous, too new.

Jake's breathing grew deep and even, the sound of an exhausted man who needed his sleep. Torey smoothed down the shirt on his back, loving to touch him, rejoicing in the privilege of doing so. She settled back on her heels, regarding him with a smile, her eyes feasting on the thick dark hair, the craggy face vulnerable now in sleep, the hard body so neatly outlined by the knit shirt and cord jeans. She reached down and slipped off the pair of deck shoes he wore, setting them beside the couch. Then, with a reluctance she battled against and won, she rose to her feet, dumped the cold coffee into the sink and turned off the light. In the silvery blue glow of the street lamp, she bent over him, touching her lips to his hair, loving the softness, the hint of lime shampoo and seabreeze there.

'Good night, Jake,' she whispered. 'Sleep well.' She let herself out, catching the nightlatch on the door as she left, her mind still remaining in the apartment, her heart fast becoming a possession of the man who lived upstairs.

'Is he back yet?' It was getting to be a ritual, Christy's voice at the door or on the 'phone as she tried unsuccessfully to track down Jake.

'Not yet,' Torey sighed, embarrassed almost by the ritual quality of her answer. For three days now she had been saying the same thing. It was as if Scott—and his father—had disappeared.

They were gone in the camper when Torey got up in the morning, and rarely did she see a light in their apartment when she went to bed at night. After three days even she couldn't tell Christy that Jake's absence was mere coincidence anymore.

'He has no right to do this,' Christy complained that afternoon when she and her fiancé, a ruggedly handsome blond, had arrived for the third time. 'I do have visitation rights.' She swept a hand through her casual hairstyle and stared helplessly at her fiancé. 'Do you want to give up, Doug?' she asked wearily, and Torey couldn't help feeling sorry for her. If Scott had meant little to her years ago, obviously that had changed now.

Doug shook his head. 'No. Not unless you do. We don't have to be back in San Francisco immediately. I'm willing to stay.' He drained the glass of iced tea that Torey had given him. 'Come on, Chris. Let's walk on the beach.'

Christy, who looked like she needed a distraction just then, obligingly followed him to the gate. Then, turning back to Torey, she said, 'I'm not leaving. I have a right to see my son. You tell him that, will you?'

'I will,' Torey promised. 'If I see him,' she added to herself. She hadn't since the night she had left him asleep on the sofa. He was avoiding her too.

'I don't understand him,' she complained to Addie. 'I mean, I know he's angry at Christy. I know he's bitter. But he's acting like a child. This running away is irrational, hysterical. What's going on in his head?'

Addie shrugged, apparently as mystified as Torey was.

It was as if he had dropped out of her life altogether. Ironic, she thought, how a month ago she would have given her eye teeth for him to do this same vanishing act. But now, when she wanted to see him, he wasn't there. 'Do you think he still loves Christy?' She asked the dreaded question, not really wanting to hear the answer. But Addie surprised her by shaking her head and saying,

'No. Though of course I'm not certain. Still, I wouldn't think so.' She cocked her head and smiled at Torey. 'Not the way he looks at you.'

Torey flushed under Addie's knowing smile, but the singing in her heart was tempered by the knowledge that Jake's passion for her had surfaced before Christy had reappeared in his life. Maybe she had merely been an adequate replacement for Christy as long as she wasn't around. But once she had come back, had Jake's old longings and memories been reawakened? She wished she knew.

By Friday she was fed up with giving Christy the same two-word response and annoyed at Jake for what she could only describe as totally irresponsible and immature behaviour. One way or another, she decided, he had to come to terms with Christy. For Torey's sake if not his own! She needed to know if he still cared for his ex-wife. She couldn't eat, she couldn't sleep. She couldn't live in this limbo he was creating by his absence. Thursday she waited until she saw a light on in his apartment and went up to knock on his door. He didn't answer it though he was obviously home.

If that's the way you want to play the game, so be it, she thought. And the following night she camped on his doorstep. He would be hard pressed to ignore her if he had to step over her to get in.

She was fortunate, she decided as she leaned against the rough stucco of the stairwell, that Manhattan Beach didn't have the mosquito population of Galena. Otherwise she'd have been eaten alive during her four-hour vigil. As it was she read a best seller, first by sunlight, and then by flashlight, until eleven thirty when she heard the truck pull in below. Snapping out the light, she huddled in the dark and waited, confident that if he got this far, he wouldn't dare turn around and walk away. She heard him kick the gate shut, then saw his silhouette as he turned the corner and ascended the stairs, Scott asleep in his arms. She waited until he was nearly to the top and fumbling for his key when she stood up and held out her hand.

'Allow me,' she said, taking the key from him and opening the door before he could protest. She preceded him into the room, switching on the lamp nearest the door, and took a look at him for the first time in five days. He was gaunt and haggard, as though he had been running a marathon without food or sleep, and angry, as though she had no right in his life. He shot her one fierce glance as he strode past her carrying Scott into his bedroom, laying him gently on his bed. Then he slipped Scott's shoes and socks off and pulled a sheet over the sleeping child.

When he came back out to the living room Torey was sitting on the couch idly flipping through an architectural digest, pretending a nonchalance she definitely didn't feel.

'We've missed you,' she remarked into the silence.

'I've been busy.'

'Running away,' she agreed calmly, pleased to see him start and then jam his fists into the pockets of his jeans.

'I am not running away.'

'Then you're doing a marvellous imitation of it.'

'Damn it, I've been working like crazy all week, taking care of Scott——'

'Instead of leaving him with us.'

'You don't want him. You said so,' he accused.

'Don't bring up arguments that we've already settled, Jake. You know perfectly well Scott is welcome. You don't want to leave him because you're afraid Christy will see him.'

Jake scowled at her. Then, when she met his blue-eyed stare with one equally firm, he dropped his head and turned his back to stare out the window into the blackness. 'So?' he growled belligerently after a long silence.

'Why?' There was no belligerence at all in Torey's voice. She could see the bleakness in his face reflected in the window and knew that driving him into a corner would gain her nothing now.

'She abandoned him,' Jake said shortly, as if she should see the obvious soundness of his actions.

'She was young then. Immature. She made a mistake. We all make mistakes, Jake,' Torey argued, wondering, even as she did so, why she was. She should be on his side! But even thinking that didn't prevent her going on. 'She's been here every day this week hoping you'll let her see Scott. She even brought her fiancé,' she added, hoping that would get a rise out of him, make him show some feeling towards Christy, whatever it might be.

But Jake didn't move. 'No.'

Stalemate. Torey stared at his T-shirt clad back, the taut muscles and stiff spine, as rigid and uncompromising as the word he just uttered. Fortunately, as she had no idea what to say next, the 'phone rang.

'Aren't you going to answer it?' she asked after the fifth ring and he still hadn't moved.

'It's probably Christy.'

'And you're not running away?' she asked scornfully, hating to hurt him.

'All right, damn it!' Jake snapped, his voice angry. He snatched the receiver up. 'Brosnan here,' he barked, and Torey hoped it wasn't Christy. After a week of no-shows from Jake, she didn't need that.

'When?' Jake was asking, his fingers lacing through his untidy hair as he wrestled with some thorny problem. An editor? Torey wondered, sure it wasn't Christy by his reaction. 'What about Mathews? Or Terry?' he asked, rubbing the back of his neck. 'Yeah, yeah. All right,' he growled and banged the 'phone down.

'Not Christy,' Torey ventured.

'The lifeguard station. They need me tomorrow and Sunday.' He looked at her bleakly, his fingers rubbing his eyes. Torey could almost see him considering his options.

'What about Scott then?' She knew what he was thinking: he couldn't take Scott while he was lifeguarding.

He shrugged. 'I don't know,' he said, chewing

his lower lip. 'Damn.'

'So why did you say you'd do it?' she pushed him. 'You don't need the money. You have been a starving artist once, but not anymore.'

'I don't do it for the money,' he said wearily.

'Why then?'

He hunched his shoulders and looked away. Torey saw his dark eyelashes blink once, heard the faucet dripping in the sink. 'Because of Mick,' he said finally, his voice hollow and low.

Mick. Torey closed her eyes, her throat tightening as she remembered Mick. Mick who had drowned, who had been Jake's best friend, who had been dating the woman who was now Jake's ex-wife. God, the tangles in their lives! She sighed, recalling Mick laughing, swigging a Coke, spiking a volleyball, talking enthusiastically about the jet planes he flew, giving her a sympathetic wink as Jake ambled past unaware. Mick with his blue eyes and white-blond hair, his sunburnt nose and cheekbones, his silvery furred legs, his flat midwestern accent not unlike Jake's. She opened her eyes and looked at Jake, catching a faraway expression on his face, a mixture of sorrow and acceptance that told her his thoughts ran along much the same lines as hers. Finally he drew a long unsteady breath and let it out slowly, saying,

'If you'll watch Scott tomorrow, if Christy comes back, you can let her see him. But you have to be there.' His voice was taut, slightly higher pitched than normal with a reedy edge to it.

Instinctively Torey rose and went to him, wrapping her arms around him, holding him gently, trying to absorb his tension and fears. 'It'll be all right,' she assured him, and wondered how she knew.

'If you say so,' Jake sighed, his cheek resting on her hair.

But she knew as she undressed for bed that night that somewhere deep down, he really didn't believe it.

*   *   *

'How would you like to be kidnapped?' Gino Martinelli asked, squatting down beside Torey's beach towel where she lay, eyes closed, listening to Scott whooping as he raced through the surf.

'Huh? Kidnapped?' Torey blinked, sitting up and taking in the wide, even grin, casually tousled hair and suggestive blue eyes peering into her own.

'Well,' she said, gathering her wits about her. 'All right. But only if I can bring the kid.'

'Kid?'

Torey nodded towards the surf line. 'Scott.'

Gino made a face. 'Attack man's son? Okay,' he conceded. 'But every time I go somewhere with you Brosnan or one of his minions comes along—in flesh or in spirit,' he grumbled. 'I thought we'd go sailing. The wind's good today. Suit you?'

'Wonderful.' She got up, calling for Scott. Jake would probably be pleased for once that she was going out with Gino. This way Scott would be gone if Christy came by. 'Just let me get dressed.' She led the way across the hot sand. 'Go play a game of Gin with my grandmother. She'll love you for it.'

Gino did, and Torey hurried into her room, whistling a nameless tune as she pulled on a pair of white cord shorts and a lemon coloured shirt over her bathing suit. Hooray for Gino, she thought as she anchored her hair with more pins than usual, even though she felt a bit guilty about removing Scott from any chance of Christy seeing him today. Still, Jake would be happy.

Or so she thought until she opened the door again and ran smack into Gino who said, 'Guess what. Scott's mother is here. She and her fiancé are coming with us too.' So much for Jake's happiness, Torey thought, her stomach knotting as she walked into the living room and came face to face with Doug. Christy was sitting on the piano bench listening raptly to Scott who was talking a mile a minute, as if his mother might disappear any second. The look in his eyes said his fondest fantasy had come true.

'She's my *mother*,' he told Torey, savouring the word like his favourite sweet.

'Hello, Christy,' Torey said, her emotions torn.

'They just got here,' Gino was saying, oblivious to all the undercurrents in the room. 'She said she hadn't seen Scott in about three years. It hardly seemed fair to take him away. So . . .' He lifted his hands expressively as if to say, 'What else could I do?' And Torey knew there wasn't anything else, so she swallowed her fears and gave Addie a peck on the cheek.

'We'll be back before five,' she promised. There was no need to say, 'Don't tell Jake.'

For all her fears, the day turned out not badly after all. Scott was eventually more enthralled with Gino's sloop than with his mother. And once he got over the initial thrill of having her there, he spent his time doing commercials for Jake.

'What a PR man,' Gino laughed as he leaned against the stern of the sloop, his arm around Torey as they listened to Scott rave about Jake's ability to swim, surf, ski, hike, draw, fish, paint, cook.

Torey saw Doug lift his brows in query as if asking Christy why, if Jake was such a superman, she had divorced him, and Christy had squeezed his arm and said, 'I love *you*, darling. Not Jake. But he is a good father,' which comforted Torey. She felt her knot of apprehension ease until Doug, his face tipped back to catch the sun, said,

'I suppose so. But it must be tough taking care of a kid, just one parent.'

'He does fine.' Torey sat up quickly and pulled away from Gino's arm. 'Fantastically well, in fact. Besides, Addie and I help him out.'

Doug didn't reply, but she had no doubt now what the real fear on Jake's horizon was. Once Doug and Christy were married, what would happen if they

decided to fight him for custody of Scott. She
remembered Jake talking about the pressures of being a
single parent the day they went to the tidepools. It must
have seemed the personification of all his fears to come
back and find Christy on his doorstep announcing that
she was marrying again. No wonder he had fled.

She gazed across the bottle green chop of the Pacific
to the wide sandy beach at Hermosa, picking out the
lifeguard towers and wondering in which one Jake was.
Or was he in the water rescuing some child? The wind
came up strongly and Scott flung himself on her, laying
his head in her lap.

'I'm sick,' he moaned, and Torey forgot Jake,
scooping up his son and holding him as Christy turned
to Doug.

'I need a bucket,' she told him and proceeded to turn
green herself.

Gino rose and began adjusting the sails. 'We'll head
back,' he said easily. 'No sense in discouraging a damn
fine crew.'

'You're a saint,' Torey said when he had them almost
back to the calm water inside the harbour. There was
no doubt that the day hadn't gone at all as he'd
planned, but he didn't seem to care. He just grinned
and pushed his white cap back on his head.

'Absolutely,' he said equably. 'When do I get my
celestial reward?' His eyes sparkled with mischief
beneath the strands of fair hair that whipped across his
face.

'In heaven,' she promised, grinning back at him.

'Brosnan's a lucky guy,' he said quietly, brushing
brotherly lips against her hair. 'A lucky guy indeed.' He
gave her a rueful smile.

Torey tilted her head, thinking about luck, about
Jake and Scott and Christy and herself, and wondering
how it would all work out. 'We'll see, Gino,' she said,
her fingers stroking Scott's soft hair as he curled in her
lap. 'We'll just have to wait and see.'

CHAPTER TEN

IT wasn't difficult to determine Jake's view of the afternoon. He was furious.

'Sailing! You took him sailing? With Christy and that ... that ... fiancé of hers?' He sounded incredulous, as if Torey had completely lost her mind and sent Scott on holiday with Jack the Ripper or something. Jake slammed his hand against Addie's kitchen cupboard and sent the dishes rattling within.

'You told me I could let her see him,' Torey reminded him quietly, not say that she hadn't even been consulted about the decision to take Christy and Doug along. What good would it do if she did?

'I thought it'd be here,' Jake stormed. 'Some place where you and Addie could keep an eye on things.'

'I was on the boat.'

'With that two-bit Casanova,' Jake fumed, crashing around the kitchen like a panther in a parlour, growling and pacing, snarling every time Torey moved. 'You were probably far too busy coming on to him to pay the least bit of attention to Scott!'

Torey stared, astonished. Had Jake taken leave of his senses? Gino? A two-bit Casanova? She almost giggled at the thought, but Jake shot her a fierce look that left her no doubt that any giggling she did would only be interpreted in the worst possible light. 'You are out of your mind,' she told him calmly, refusing even to jump at the bait of his insistence that she must have been 'coming on' to Gino. Another time she might have clobbered him for making that assumption. Now she suspected that he was so overwrought that he had no idea of what he was saying. Or at least she hoped he didn't.

'You're damned right I'm out of my mind,' he snarled. 'With half of LA County down at the beach today trying to drown themselves, I didn't need this.'

'Bad day, huh?' Torey asked, going to put the kettle on. Perhaps a cup of tea and a little sympathy would accomplish what rationality didn't seem able to at the moment. At least she needed to get him calmed down before he saw Scott. Any descriptions Scott gave Jake of his mother and Doug were likely to be enthusiastic, and Torey sensed that Jake's present frame of mind was not conducive to receiving such reports with equanimity.

'A very bad day,' he agreed. 'I doused fifty or so people with ammonia for jelly fish stings, took one to the hospital for a shock reaction to the stings, removed a fish hook from a three-year-old's foot, dragged thirty or so "swimmers"—and I use the term loosely—out of a riptide, broke up a brawl between a bunch of young thugs arguing over a supposedly stolen surfboard, and carried another kid to the hospital after a surfing accident.' He sank down in one of the chairs and rested his elbows on the table, cradling his head in his hands. Then he looked up, his chin in his hands, his eyes a stormy sea. 'And now you tell me that you've taken Scott out sailing with my dear ex-wife.'

'She has visitation rights, Jake,' Torey reminded him even though she felt a tug of sympathy for him. The kettle whistled and she made the pot of tea, keeping her back to him but sensing that his eyes were on her all the while.

'She never wanted them until now,' Jake said bitterly.

Torey poured a cup of tea and carried it across to him, setting it on the table as she said, 'But now she does. And you have to let her.'

'Why do I?' He was scowling into his cup like an angry child.

'Because he is her son. Honestly Jake, you're acting like a little boy with a toy he won't share. If you don't let her see him at least part of the time, she may decide to try to get him all the time.'

Jake jerked his head up, his face suddenly pale. 'Custody?' he asked hoarsely. 'Did she say that?'

'No,' Torey admitted. But she remembered what Doug had implied about one-parent families. The conclusion was an easy jump.

'You don't sound very sure,' he pressed. 'What did she say?'

'Nothing really. I don't know that she would. But if you were my ex-husband trying to keep my son from me, I know what I'd do,' she told him.

'You don't understand,' he muttered, his head bent over his tea, the words almost lost in the cup.

'No, I don't,' Torey said slowly. 'They are truly nice people, Jake. I don't know what happened during your marriage. I'm sure it must not have been easy, but Christy doesn't seem to be evil through and through. If you don't give her a chance to see Scott on your terms, she may try to take him away from you.'

'Damn.' His voice was low, shot through with a pain that Torey could not completely comprehend. There was so much about what had happened to him when he was married to Christy that she didn't understand, that no one had ever explained to her. All she could see was the present—the pain and tension of a little boy about to be torn two ways. She wanted to comfort Jake but she didn't know how. He had locked that part of himself off from her. She knew that the last five years had been hard, that he had brought up his son basically on his own, had been both mother and father to Scott and loved him more than life itself. And she knew that now his world was being threatened, or he thought that it was. But she didn't see any way to help. If only she knew more about his relationship with Christy, then maybe she could. Or at least she might be better able to understand the passion with which he opposed Christy having anything more to do with their child.

Jake picked up the cup again and drained the rapidly cooling tea, then set it down with the finality of a condemned man. 'I have to guard again tomorrow,' he said heavily. 'Will you watch Scott again?'

'Yes, of course. What if Christy and Doug come?'

Jake sighed and rubbed his hand across his eyes. 'I don't know,' he mumbled. 'I just don't know.' He shoved back the chair and got to his feet, straightening up one vertebrae at a time as though the effort were almost too much for him. 'Send Scott home for supper, will you?' he said as an afterthought as he went out the door. 'G'night.'

Goodnight? Torey stared after him worried. It wasn't even six o'clock. But Jake was shambling across the yard with the demeanour of a boxer whose gone several rounds too long. There was none of his confident swagger left. He looked completely defeated and, as far as she knew, so far there hadn't even been a fight.

When Torey poked her head out of her bedroom the next morning it was to find Addie and Scott stirring up a cake. 'What's the occasion?' she asked as she paused to ruffle Scott's hair.

'It's Jake's birthday,' Addie explained as she poured the batter into two round pans and motioned for Torey to open the oven door.

'An' we're makin' him a cake. Chocolate,' Scott said through a smeared grin. ''Cause it's his favourite.'

'Mine too. How *is* Jake?' Torey asked her grandmother who pursed her lips and said,

'Tired by the look of him.'

'He was up real late,' Scott chimed in. 'We went to get Lola last night.'

Shaken Torey looked at him across the table. 'You went to get Lola?' Since Christy had arrived on the scene she had forgotten there was another woman in Jake's life. Had he needed a woman's solace last night?

With a stab of jealousy Torey imagined that he might. She certainly hadn't offered any.

'Yeah. We jus' took her home this morning before he went to guard. Usually I don't get to go pick her up,' Scott went on. 'Usually I stay with Addie.'

But not last night. Last night Jake was keeping Scott close. Did he think that Christy might show up again in the evening and try to see Scott if he left him with Addie? 'Well, you're here now,' she said lightly, knowing that there was nothing more to learn about Lola from Scott. 'What shall we do today?'

'Go buy Dad a present,' Scott suggested.

'Yes, do,' Addie seconded. 'There's an art book I know he wants. Could you get it for him from me?'

'Sure. We'll go right after the cake is out,' Torey said. 'We can make a day of it, have lunch out if you want,' she told Scott.

'Neato!' Scott bounced off his chair and tossed the spoon he was licking into the sink, dashing out before Addie could collar him and run a damp cloth over his chocolate smeared face. 'You're super, Torey!' he called back.

'And what if Christy comes while you're out?' Addie asked, completely aware of what Torey was doing before Torey even knew it herself.

Torey shrugged. 'She saw him yesterday. Besides, it won't be any different than if Jake had him somewhere else,' she defended herself. She wasn't entirely comfortable with what she was doing, knowing that it was going to aid Jake in his effort to keep Scott away from his mother. But she couldn't help, either, how she felt about Jake. He had given five years of his life to caring for and supporting his son. If he felt so strongly that Christy shouldn't have access to him, even though Torey herself might not understand why, she wanted it the way he did. 'If she comes tell her we'll be back shortly after lunch,' Torey compromised.

She was dressing for their shopping expedition when

the phone rang. 'If it's for me,' she called, 'I'll be right out.' But Addie didn't answer so Torey finished plaiting her hair and slipped her feet into a pair of huaraches.

'It's the lifeguard station,' Addie said, opening her door. 'They want you to come and get Jake.'

Torey felt a shiver slice down her spine. In her mind she saw Dave Sorenson's face the afternoon he came to the door, white and drawn, and told her what had happened to Paul. 'What is it?'

'He's been stung.'

'Stung?'

Addie shrugged. 'A jelly fish sting, that's what they said. Or several of them. They seemed in a rush. Just come and get him, they said.'

A jelly fish sting? Torey wanted to laugh with relief. 'Can't he drive?' she asked, incredulous.

'I don't know. Call them back and ask, if you want.'

Torey did, stunned at what she heard. 'He sounds very ill,' she told her grandmother. 'Shock, the man said. Lord, where's my bag?' Her eyes scanned the room seeing nothing. 'I'll call a cab to take me down. I can drive him home in his truck.'

'What did they say then?' Addie wanted to know, her expression darkening as she watched her granddaughter scramble for a phone book.

'Something about multiple stings and allergic reaction. I remember Jake saying that he took a man to the hospital for that. Why didn't they take him to the hospital?' She was thumbing through the directory, forgetting the alphabet and beginning again.

'Hey Addie,' Scott hollered coming up the back steps. 'My Mom is here.'

'Oh swell,' Torey muttered. 'Not now, God. Please not now.'

But sure enough Torey looked up to see Scott with Christy and Doug right behind him.

'We're going to get Dad a birthday present,' Scott was telling them.

'Not right now,' Torey corrected, her finger finally locating the cabs.

'Why?' Scott wailed.

'Your dad's been hurt. I have to go get him.'

'What happened?' Doug asked.

'Jelly fish sting,' Torey told him, beginning to dial. 'I'm calling a cab to go get him.'

'I'll take you,' Doug offered.

Torey stopped dialling and looked at Doug indecisively. Jake would want her to take a cab. But who knew how long it would take a cab to get here. 'All right,' she decided.

'But we gotta get him his present,' Scott insisted.

'Your dad won't care about a present,' Torey said, but Christy cut in,

'We'll drop Torey off and take you out to get the present, Scott.'

'Yeah!' Scott beamed, threatened tears vanishing.

'But . . .' Torey fumbled knowing what Jake would think.

'We won't be gone long,' Doug assured her, obviously sensing her fears. 'Just shopping, lunch and home. Three hours at most.'

'Well . . .' Torey looked at Addie but her grandmother was impassive. No help there.

'For God's sake,' Doug said impatiently. 'We're not kidnapping the boy if that's what you're worried about. Christy's his mother!'

Torey saw the very thing she had warned Jake about building up inside Doug right now. There was a hint of resolve, a hardening. He would not hesitate to challenge Jake's right to Scott, she knew it. There was going to have to be some giving done, and she would have to do it. 'All right,' she said. 'Thanks. I appreciate the offer of a lift.' She didn't know what she would tell Jake. There would be time enough later to think about that.

In fact all thought of explanation fled the moment she saw Jake. He was lying on a narrow cot, his eyes shut, his face ashen. She didn't hear a word the lifeguard lieutenant was saying to her, instead rushing across the room to kneel beside Jake. Her voice shook as she called his name. 'Jake! Jake!'

Jake's eyelids flickered open. At first he didn't seem to focus on her, his eyes a blue haze of pain and disorientation. Then, when he did, he managed a grimace more aching than wry for once. Then his eyes closed again.

Torey looked up at the tall man in navy blue pants and shirt who was hovering over them. 'What's wrong with him? Why is he like this?'

'He was rescuing a man who had been stung. Getting him out wasn't easy, and the jelly fish had a heyday. Jake has welts all over his thighs and chest.' The man shook his head in disbelief.

'Shouldn't he go to a hospital?'

'I suggested it. Jake didn't want to. We did have a doctor here to check him over. He gave me a prescription you can have filled.' He handed it to her. 'Not much else we can do now. He'll be all right. Just take him home and put him to bed.'

Easier said than done, Torey thought as she and the lieutenant wrestled Jake out to the truck. His teeth were chattering and his breathing was shallow. She wasn't at all sure that she ought to accept charge of him. What if he died? The lieutenant didn't seem to have any such qualms. He shut the door to the truck saying cheerfully, 'See you next week,' as though ashen-faced, teeth-rattling lifeguards were the norm in his life. Jake didn't answer.

Torey couldn't blame him.. He looked barely conscious, his head resting on the glass of the door window as she hastily extricated the truck from its parking place and began the trek homeward.

He groaned once and she shot him a swift glance. 'Do you hurt a lot?'

'Yes.' The answer was barely audible. Torey stepped

on the accelerator. She didn't think about Scott again until she pulled into the garage and had to make the decision of whether to take Jake to his own apartment or bring him to Addie's. His own place won. The chance of him discovering that Christy had taken Scott out were much greater if he went to Addie, and far more than she imagined he could take at the moment.

With minimal help from Jake she dragged him up the stairs, overwhelmingly conscious of his virile length pressed against her own, his arm slung heavily over her shoulders, his hair brushing against her ear as they climbed. Thank God for her training as a physico-therapist. Being used to bodies in all states carried her through. She set her mind on automatic pilot as she helped him into the bedroom, removed the thin blanket that he had wrapped around his shoulders and, laying him down on the bed, stripped off his still damp swim trunks. It was more of Jake Brosnan than she had ever seen, and even automatic pilot couldn't stop her pulse racing and the lump growing in her throat as she tugged the trunks down over his hips and thighs, being careful to keep the fabric away from the reddish purple welts that were his souvenirs of the jelly fish stings.

'Not exactly the scenario I had in mind,' Jake whispered, a ghost of a grin flickering across his face.

'Me neither,' Torey said, busying herself by taking his trunks into the bathroom and tossing them in the shower. She'd had plenty of wild fantasies about Jake, but none came close to this. 'Is that ammonia I smell?' she asked him when she came back, her eyes avoiding his lean torso.

'Yeah. Ross said sometimes baking powder or flour helps too,' he told her, quoting the unconcerned lieutenant. 'Something about changing the pH of the skin.'

'Want some?' she asked, wondering what she would do if he did.

'I guess. Hurts like sin right now.' One hand came up

and brushed lightly over his chest and he gritted his teeth as it did so. 'Boy, I sure don't remember any stings quite like this one before.'

'You've got so many. That must be why.' She wiped damp palms on her jeans and went to find the baking powder. There was none. Not surprising, she thought, you didn't need that to make bread. But there was a ten-pound sack of flour in the cupboard so she scooped some out into a bowl and came back, struggling to make herself feel detached and professional while she dusted the white powder all over the welts on his body. Jake lay still under her ministrations, fingers clenching the sheet. His eyes followed her every move, boring into her, hot and steady, so that her hand trembled and she spilled flour on the sheet. 'Damn,' she muttered. Then, finishing, 'Now what?'

Jake shrugged. 'Some say scrape it off, some leave it on.'

'We'll leave it on,' Torey decided. There was no way she was going to run her hands over him one more time with impunity. Not and keep up any pretence of indifference!

'Is Scott with Addie?' he asked as she moved to carry the bowl back to the kitchen.

'Um,' she mumbled, crossing her fingers and hoping she was telling the truth. 'I'll keep an eye on him. You sleep now.' She set the bowl on the bar and went back to draw a sheet over him, taking as she did so her first real look around his bedroom. It was a far cry from the playboy's seduction parlour of her imaginings. The bed was a double one to be sure, but chances were it was left over from the days of his marriage to Christy. It was made up in serviceable white muslin sheets with a thin brown cotton spread identical to the one in Scott's room flung over a nearby chair. The books, far from being the erotic literature she had once supposed, tended towards art books, architecture digests, marine biology and mystery fiction. Not a *Playboy* or

Penthouse in sight. The room was overrun with sketching materials, bottles of ink, artist's separations and dirty laundry. If he entertained Lola or any other woman in this room it would be less to seduce them, she decided, than to coerce them into cleaning it up and doing his washing. Absently, almost the way she had picked up after Paul, she scooped up a pile of grimy T-shirts and a pair of paint-spattered jeans and tucked them under her arm.

'I'll be back shortly,' she told Jake. But Jake hadn't heard. His eyes were closed, his breathing shallow but even, his hands relaxed on top of the sheet.

She took his laundry down and put it in Addie's washer. 'Is Scott back?'

'Not yet. How's Jake?'

'They say he'll be fine.' Torey poured in soap and bleach, considered the greyish shirts and added a dollop more. 'But you couldn't prove it by me. I think he looks awful. He's asleep now. I just came down to do this laundry.'

'I'll finish it,' Addie said. 'You go on back up with Jake.'

Since this was exactly what Torey wanted to do, she didn't offer any protest, only said, 'Let me know when Scott gets back will you. I want to head him off at the pass. Poor Jake, what a birthday!'

If there were any way it could be more miserable, Torey couldn't imagine it. When she got back he was still asleep, but not the peaceful sleep she would have hoped for. He twisted on the bed, tangling in the sheet, his fingers clenching and unclenching, then rubbing at his chest and legs. His dark hair clung damply to his forehead, and Torey ran her hand under it, lifting it off and feeling the heat of his body against her hand. He muttered something, but didn't wake so she crept quietly back to the living room and made herself a cup of coffee. Then she read a mystery while she waited for him to wake.

It could have been an hour or even two, she was dozing on the sofa when she heard the 'phone ring and feet pounding on the stairs at the same moment. Torn, she opted for the 'phone and heard Addie say, 'Scott's on his way. I'm not fast enough on my feet any more.'

The front door burst open and Scott ran into the room waving a package in Torey's face.

'Scott?' Jake's weak voice came from the bedroom.

'Never mind,' Torey said to her grandmother, trying to put herself between Scott and the bedroom. 'Too late now. See you later.' She hung up.

'Hey, Dad! Happy birthday! I got you the neatest present ever!' There was no slowing down a five-year-old tornado, Torey decided. All she could do was cross her fingers and pray that he concentrated on the present and not on how Scott got it.

Jake was up on his elbows in bed, the sheet down around his waist leaving exposed the flour smudged chest and bronzed shoulders. 'Birthday present?' he echoed dumbly, as though he wasn't quite with it yet.

'Are you all right now?' Torey looped her arms around Scott and held him captive so that he couldn't fling himself on to his father in his excitement.

'I think so,' Jake stretched his torso, arching his back. The sheet slipped further and Torey caught her breath. 'Doesn't hurt so much. No more muscle cramps either. I guess I'll live.'

Torey smiled, her heart beating faster. 'Good.'

'Here, Dad,' Scott said, wiggling out of her arms to run to his father and thrust a package in his face. 'Open it.'

Jake sat up, shooting an oblique look at Torey as he did so and making an obvious effort to keep the sheet anchored modestly around his hips. He set the package on his lap and began to remove the cellophane tape. 'When did you go shopping?' he asked now, his eyes still on Torey.

'Oh, um, well . . .' She should have known her sins would find her out.

'Torey was gonna take me when you got stung,' Scott told him. 'She couldn't go, so my mom and my new dad did instead.'

Jake's face went chalk white, his throat working so convulsively that Torey thought he might gag. 'New dad?' He sounded wretched.

'My mom is marrying him so he's a sort of a dad,' Scott explained as though Jake needed it spelled out. 'Isn't he?' he looked confused. 'A stairdad?'

'Stepdad,' Torey corrected gently. Her eyes were on Jake, she wanted to touch him, hold him, protect him from the anguish Scott's words were causing him. He looked as though he had been slapped.

'*They* took him?' His eyes levelled on Torey accusingly, the pain harsh in his face.

'Yes.' There was no way to lie about it or soften it. 'I had to come and get you or I would have taken him. Scott was terribly disappointed. Christy and Doug came by just then and volunteered. They even dropped me off at the station to pick you up.' Her eyes locked with his, half duelling, half imploring. She knew he was devastated, but she also knew that Scott needed some reassurance just now that he hadn't completely let Jake down. He was hanging on the edge of the dresser looking from one to the other of them, his eyes wide and worried. 'Come on, Jake,' she wanted to say. Scream at me later if you must, but don't take it out on your son.

'Open the present, Jake,' she urged. 'Let's see your neat gift.'

Jake seemed to have to will his fingers to move. With excruciating slowness he stripped the remaining paper off the box and prised off the lid. Inside were three tissue wrapped smaller packages. Scott hopped from one foot to the other, his eyes shining and apprehensive.

Jake took the smallest package and unwrapped it. There, in his hand, lay a tiny green ceramic dragon with a long tail that looked real enough to begin twitching and a broad grin on its face. Torey saw Jake blink and draw a deep breath before saying shakily, 'You found me a dragon.'

'Yup.' Scott was practically dancing with excitement now. 'Open the rest, Dad!'

With hands that trembled just the slightest bit, Jake did. When he had finished there were three dragons sitting in the tissue paper nest in his lap. He didn't say a word. Couldn't, Torey would have guessed. His fingers stroked each of them almost absently as though his mind were far away.

'See. There's three of 'em.' Scott beamed at him. 'Like for your book. A father, a mother and a kid. A family.'

'A family.' Jake's voice was dull and aching. It pained Torey just to hear it. Tears pricked behind her eyes as she stared at the little dragon family and remembered how Jake had drawn her as a dragon. The mother dragon? 'Thanks,' he said. It sounded as though he had dragged the words up from his toes. Scott, fortunately, heard only the word, not the emotions crowded into it.

'That's why I had to go with Mom and Doug,' he told Jake. 'I wouldn't have been able to get you such a great present otherwise.' He reached out and touched the middle sized dragon on Jake's knee. 'Can I take 'em down and show 'em to Addie?'

'Sure.' Jake managed a smile and reached out to touch Scott's hair. Seconds later the door banged and Scott was gone.

Into the silence Torey said, 'I'm sorry, Jake. About him going with Christy. But he did want to get you a present.' It sounded lame and inadequate, but she had to say something.

'Some present.' Jake's voice was hollow. His hand brushed the tissue paper to the floor and he sank back against the pillow, rolling on to his side away from her. 'Some present,' he muttered again. 'Losing my son.'

Had he? Was the dragon family that Scott wanted to mirror his own, one in which Christy and Doug would be the parents and Jake would have no part? No! she wanted to cry. No, Scott was Jake's son! No one could deny him his child, not after five years of love and care just because Scott's mother was now ready to accept him into her new life. Torey sighed wishing she was sure of that. She went down and got his laundry from Addie, returning immediately so she wouldn't have to listen to Scott regale Addie with stories of his afternoon out. Jake was lying in bed, silent and unmoving, and there was nothing more she could say, so she left him alone. She began folding the laundry, mechanically smoothing out the small T-shirts that were Scott's and piling them alongside Jake's larger ones. The Jack Daniel's Whiskey one was in the heap and she brought it up against her cheek, thinking again about the first time she had seen him this summer after seven long years. God, how she had fought against her renewed attraction to him! How different he seemed from the tender, gentle, loving husband she had had in Paul. Even now, she knew, he was different. He was moodier than Paul, mercurial, gifted. But he had a solid core of responsibility too. He might not be the steady, uncomplaining, always smiling man that Paul had been, but he was just as strong and dependable in his own way. If he wasn't the romantic hero she had once imagined him, the epitome of handsome wickedness just waiting for her to love and reform him, he was still the man whom, without trying, without even wanting to, she had come to love again.

Whether Jake was sleeping because he was exhausted or whether it was a way to avoid the problems of his life, he still made a good job of it. He slept right through dinner which was a can of ravioli for Torey while Scott and Addie had meat loaf downstairs. They ate birthday cake without him, and by Scott's bedtime he was still not awake.

'Will you keep Scott down here tonight?' Torey asked

her grandmother when she came down to get her own nightgown, and receiving an affirmative reply, she went back to Jake's place and settled in to spend the night. She first heard him fumbling his way to the kitchen as the digital clock on Scott's dresser read 2:56. Drawing a thin cotton robe on over her nightgown, Torey scrambled out of bed and walked noiselessly into the dark living room. 'How are you feeling?'

Jake flinched as though he'd been shot. Spinning around, he stared across the room in the direction of her voice. 'You're still here?'

'Of course. You didn't really think I'd leave when you were hurt, did you?'

Jake shrugged, coming around from behind the bar where he had been standing so that she could see his face and bare chest more clearly in the spill of silvery moonlight through the windows.

'I thought you'd have quit me long ago,' he said slowly, coming to stop about a foot in front of her, near enough so that she could distinguish the dark whorls of hair on his chest and caught the faint smell of ammonia in the air. Her eyes dropped. Another mistake. He was still as bare as he had been after she took his swimming trunks off that afternoon. Quickly, heart hammering, she sought his face again.

'No,' she said. 'I'm still here. Do you feel bad again?'

There was a heavy silence between them. Then Jake sighed. 'Yeah.'

'Do the stings still bother you? Can I give you one of the pills?'

'No. It's not that.' He stared at her, then with noticeable reluctance, he moved around her to go towards the bedroom.

'Is it Scott?' She turned to watch his back and saw the slumped line of his shoulders.

He stopped, dark head bent. 'Yeah.' Then he padded into the bedroom and she heard the springs creak as he lay back down on his bed. For a full minute she hung suspended like a marionette, trying to decide if she should follow him or leave him alone with his misery. He was not, after all, asking for sympathy. He wasn't asking her for anything. But she couldn't let him go on like this. If it was Scott bothering him, he needed to think realistically about what he was going to do with Christy in his life again. He had to learn to let go of Scott. Even just a tiny bit.

'Jake,' she said, decision made. She went to the door of his room and peered in at him huddled in the bed in the darkness. 'I don't think you'll lose Scott. Truly, I don't. But you can't smother him either. You can't protect him against all contact with his mother.'

'I'm not protecting him,' Jake growled, and she saw him pull himself up to a sitting position, his dark shape looming in the bed.

'Well, you act like it. Why are you keeping him away from her then?'

'You wouldn't understand.'

'Try me.'

Silence.

She moved nearer to the bed, then sat on the edge of it, her hip pressing against Jake's knee. 'Do you still love her?' she asked tightly, fearing what the answer would be.

'Love Christy?' That seemed to floor him. 'God, no, I never did!'

Torey pulled back, stunned. 'Then why did you marry . . .' Stupid, stupid question, she told herself at once. Why did all sorts of people get married? Babies. Children like Scott. Christy had been pregnant. Torey felt her cheeks grow warm, but she stumbled on. 'But then, if you don't love her, why do you care if she marries Doug? Just because of the custody thing?'

Minutes seemed to pass before he answered. Torey held her breath until she heard his barely audible, 'Yes.'

'But you've had Scott all his life,' she argued. 'You could say that in a court hearing. You could tell them how she left you. Natural fathers have a lot of rights these days.'

'Yes,' Jake agreed softly. 'They do. But naturally speaking, Scott is not my son.'

'What?'

Jake shifted in the bed, drawing his knees up and wrapping his arms around them, pulling himself together like a turtle into his shell. 'You knew Christy when she was dating Mick, didn't you?'

'Yes.'

'Scott is Mick's child. Christy was pregnant with him when Mick was killed.' His voice was muffled against his wrist. 'I don't think he even knew it. There were a bunch of us out surfing. It was a wild day, high wind, steep breakers. We'd driven down to Laguna. The surf curls tighter there. Or it did that day.' His words were coming slowly as if he were pulling them out, one by one, as he made himself relive the pain of it. Torey ached to stop him, but she couldn't. She had to know it all if she were ever going to help him, and she sensed that, to face Christy again, he would have to work it through again himself.

'We were the last ones coming in, Mick and I,' he went on. 'Christy and some other girl were waiting for us on the beach. I——' his voice cracked here. 'I challenged M-Mick to one last ride.' His body tensed with pain and Torey's fingers closed around the calf of his leg, needing to share his anguish. 'I came in without a scratch. Mick fell and knocked himself out. He drowned.' Jake bent his head, resting it on his arm, his fingers twisted, knotting the sheet, and Torey felt a sob tear through him. She kneaded the muscles of his calf, her heart aching for him. For Mick.

'Three days after Mick was buried, Christy came to my place and said she was pregnant with Mick's baby. She wanted me to give her the money for an abortion. She couldn't raise a kid alone, she said. Besides, she figured I owed it to her.' His mouth curved in a smile of bitter self-recrimination and she shook her head in despair. 'I couldn't give it to her. I *wouldn't* give it to her. I felt responsible enough for Mick's death. I wasn't about to destroy his child.' He sighed heavily. 'So I said no to the abortion. I told her she didn't have to raise the kid alone, I'd marry her.' He shrugged and laced his fingers together. 'What choice did she have then? She agreed.'

'So you got married and had Scott.' Torey's mind was reeling.

'Yeah. But Christy never loved me, nor I her. It was expedient, that's all. She didn't like being tied down and, once Scott was born, she didn't like me for having forced wife-and-motherhood on her. So she went back to work and I kept Scott. Three years ago she got disgusted with even that. I can't blame her. I was wrong to force her to marry me. But I didn't see any other way out. Not to be fair to Mick and his child. God, I love that child!' His eyes were pools of misery and despair.

'I know.' Torey inched up the side of the bed and put her other hand on his shoulder, needing to touch him, to show him that she understood.

'But,' he said heavily, 'I know, intellectually at least, that you're right. Christy is not a bad person. And I think in her way, especially now, she probably does love Scott. And now that she's getting married, for love this time,' his voice caught on the last phrase, 'I think she may try to take him away from me.'

'But you're still his legal father.'

'Legal father, moral father, everything but his natural father,' Jake intoned grimly. 'I'm also a single father. And we both know the limitations to that. Hell,' he sighed, rubbing a weary hand against the back of his neck. 'I ought to get married too. At least then if she challenges me for custody, I'll have a fighting chance.'

Torey thought he was joking, but he didn't look it. There was a crazy light of desperation in his eyes. Marriage? Was he serious? Her heart started speeding as she considered it. It was crazy really, wasn't it? To get married just to hang on to Scott? 'Jake?' she whispered tremulously, and he turned his head to face her. For an eternity neither of them moved. Then, as if the cord which had confined him had snapped, Jake reached for her, his arms going around her with the desperation of a drowning man, pulling her back down with him on the bed.

Torey, too, felt something snap. She had kept her emotions reined in all the time she had listened, letting him spill out all his pain unhampered while she had longed to comfort and shush him. But now, in his arms, all thoughts of restraint vanished. Her hands moved feverishly over his body, learning the muscles of his back, the planes of his chest, outlining his neck and shoulders. Her fingers threaded themselves through the silky softness of his hair, stroking and twining, making him moan with pleasure.

But the pleasure was not all his. Jake, too, was feverish, demanding, almost desperate as his fingers fumbled with the snaps on her robe, dragging it apart with haste and tossing it on the floor only to encounter her nightgown. 'God, so many layers,' he complained hoarsely as he nibbled with exquisite tenderness on the lobe of her ear.

Laughing silently, Torey drew back enough to allow him to ease the nightgown over her head. Then his shaking hands were curving down her bare torso in the dim silvery blue moonlight. She shivered under his gaze, an artist's gaze, seeing more of her than she thought possible in the shadowy darkness of the room. Just the look on his face caused her to smoulder. But when he bent down, his hands shaping her breasts and lifting them to receive his mouth, she thought she would burst into flame.

'Jake,' she murmured, tugging at his head, trying to bring his mouth up to hers, to ease the delightful sensations he was creating, to dampen the flames coursing throughout her body. But Jake would have none of it. His mouth roamed lower, nibbling, caressing, traversing her ribs, then easing slowly up towards her breasts again. Torey trapped him by hooking her leg around his, causing them both to lose their balance and tumble off the bed on to the thickly carpeted floor.

'Glad we don't have downstairs neighbours,' Jake murmured just before his mouth fastened over hers, his tongue slipping between her parted teeth, stroking lightly against hers.

But Torey wasn't thinking of neighbours. Her universe had shrunk to the size of one man. He was all that mattered, and she wrapped her arms around the warmth of his body, drawing him down on to her, into her, shuddering at the feeling of exquisite rightness. She felt him shaking, moving ever more quickly, his breath coming in gasps just as hers was. Her heart seemed to expand, pressing against the walls of her chest, and she dug her nails into his back until finally the flames exploded into one great bonfire consuming them both.

The fire quenched, Torey lay quietly, her eyes closed, her mind centred on the glorious feeling of Jake's body, damp and heavy, warm on top of her own. As her breath slowed, she drew one hand up in almost slow motion and stroked gently down the length of his back.

Jake let out a long deep breath. 'Wow.' A quiet laugh shook his chest. 'That was definitely worth waiting seven years for!' He lifted his head off her shoulder to look down into her eyes.

Was it? she wanted to ask. Had she pleased him as much as she had been pleased? Did he love her as she loved him? There were a million questions, all of them needing answers, and she couldn't bring herself to ask a single one. Instead she smiled at him, offering him her heart with her eyes. 'Yes,' she said softly, reaching up to draw his lips down to touch hers. 'Yes.'

This time their lovemaking was leisurely, a lingering

exploration that teased and titillated their senses and which bore little resemblance to their first desperate union. Jake took his time, loving her as she had always imagined he would love, giving himself to her just as she gave herself to him. And when, once more, they had consummated their passion in a storm of summer lightning, Torey slept secure and warm, home at last in Jake's strong arms.

She awoke early, the morning sun on Jake's face causing him to shift his head to find a shaded spot on her shoulder to rest his head. The events and revelations of the night before came back in a rush. But above all she knew that this man next to her was the man she loved. With her eyes she traced the line of his jaw, the bump of his once broken nose, the dark hair that feathered across his forehead, and knew that, far from being the strong man always in control of every situation, Jake was just as vulnerable and needful of true love and understanding as she was. And she wanted to be the person to love him. She wanted to be the one to help him keep Scott. If she married him she could do both.

In the clear morning light the thought of marrying Jake struck her to the core. Like a dangerous animal, the issue of marriage to Jake had been one she had avoided ever seriously thinking about. There was too much temptation to indulge in wishful thinking, in romantic pipedreaming. But it was no pipedream that Jake had been talking about last night. He had talked about marriage as a necessity, as a means of keeping Scott in his home, and suddenly Torey knew that now was the time to face the dangerous animal head-on.

Ever since Paul's death she had been thinking about her own life, her own happiness. Even when she had been dating—or avoiding—Harlan and Vince, it hadn't been them she was concerned about. No, she had always been too busy protecting herself from involvement, always trying to make sure that the love she gave was on her own terms where she stood the least chance of being hurt. She had never given anyone else's needs a thought.

Least of all, Jake's. But now she did because she loved him. He was as much a part of her life as Paul had ever been, however different they might be. And her love of him was on no one's terms. It was an overwhelming, overriding passion which knew no reason other than to give itself to him. And if she married him, things would come right for him—he would get to keep Scott and, if he didn't really love her now the way she loved him, at least he had a start on it. The look in his eyes last night proved that. It would work out, she knew it would!

Smiling she leaned over and kissed his cheek, rubbing her lips against his dark stubble, drinking in the smell of ammonia and seawater and that indefinable essence that could only be called Jake. Sleepily he opened his eyes, the same colour as the ocean on a sunlit morning, and saw her smiling at him. Slowly, ever so tentatively, he smiled back.

'You know, Jake,' she said softly, her eyelashes brushing against his nose. 'You might have a good idea there—that business about getting married to keep Scott.'

She felt him tense beneath her. 'Oh?' The ocean blue eyes narrowed warily as he studied her.

Torey lifted herself away from him, feeling like an idiot, wishing she had written out her dialogue ahead of time so it wouldn't sound so inane when she said it. 'I mean, I'd marry you,' she offered. God, no wonder men didn't like to propose.

Jake blinked as if he thought he might not be awake. 'You'd marry me?' He sounded stunned.

'Yes.'

The silence lasted an eternity.

'No,' he said.

CHAPTER ELEVEN

THE bottom fell out of her world. 'No?'

Jake shook his head, avoiding her eyes. 'No.' He sat up and hauled himself out of bed, groping around on the drafting table for a pair of jeans, his movements harsh and jerky. 'I married once for the wrong reasons. It was a mess from beginning to end. I'll never do it again.' He found the jeans and a pair of underpants and hastily stepped into them, zipping them up and running a nervous hand through his dishevelled dark hair. He still wouldn't meet her eyes.

Just as well, Torey thought mortified. She found her robe on the floor and tugged it on, snapping it with trembling fingers as though she could camouflage her body, as though there were parts of it he hadn't seen! How could he have just said, 'No,' in such a flat cold voice when last night they had shared something so beautiful? Well, perhaps to Jake it hadn't been beautiful, maybe it was only a need to be assuaged. So much for her ability to interpret the look in his eyes. Surely such a blatant refusal was a terrific indication that he didn't really love her.

Scrambling out of the bed she hurried into Scott's room where she had left her clothes, calling over her shoulder, 'I'm glad you're better then. I'll just be on my way.' Hot tears threatened to spill on to the carpet and she blinked them back furiously, swallowing the tight lump in her throat. God, talk about idiots! How could she have been so stupid as to offer herself like that? Her hands shook as she dressed and used Scott's tiny comb to do a barely passable job on her hair. A glance in the mirror showed her a pale face with smudge rimmed eyes, a face she recognised from the early days after

170

Paul's death. Quickly she looked away, rolling her robe into a ball and looking about for her nightgown. Damn, she had left it in Jake's room. Well, she certainly wasn't going to go back for it. He could just add it to his souvenir collection. Maybe he'd see it and think of her sometime!

'Hang on,' he said, coming out of his bedroom buttoning up his shirt as she crossed the living room towards the door.

'What?' She didn't stop walking.

He moved to intercept her, nearly knocking over the chair between them. 'I—I just wanted to say thanks,' he said in a low voice, his eyes watching his bare toes with all-consuming interest.

Torey stopped and glared. 'Thanks?' Her voice was high and shrill. 'Thanks for what? Coming to get you? Pouring flour all over you? Sitting up with you? Going to bed with you? Making a fool of myself? Forget it! It's all part of the service!'

He lifted his hand to grab her arm but she jerked away, wrenching open the door and bolting down the stairs, leaving him white and ill-tempered in her wake.

'What's wrong?' Addie asked the moment she set eyes on her granddaughter.

'Nothing.' Torey swiped a hand across her eyes and headed for her bedroom, face averted.

'Scott's still sleeping in there,' Addie's voice drifted after her.

Damn. She opened the door quietly, tossed her robe on the dresser and went back to the living room. 'I'm going out for a walk,' she told Addie, her eyes busy memorising the roses on the front hallway carpet.

'Long night was it?' Addie clucked sympathetically.

'Very.' An understatement if there ever was one.

'How's Jake?'

'Back to normal.' That was the truth at least. Torey turned and opened the door, needing to escape any more questions just then. 'I'll be back in a while,' she said, knowing that Addie could hear the break in her voice and not even caring.

She walked quickly down the pavement to the sand and jumped over the low wall to the beach. What had he said? 'I married once for the wrong reasons.' Well, that certainly spelled it out in no uncertain terms. He hadn't loved Christy by his own admission, and obviously he didn't love her either. Torey felt her heart tighten as she walked, the loose sand underfoot easier going than the emotional sand she was struggling through. She had been a fool to offer herself to him that way, a fool to think that they might make a good marriage just because she had come to love him. 'I'd marry you,' she had said. God, she cringed now at the thought, her cheeks burning with mortification at the remembrance of her fumbling, ill-worded attempt to give him her life and her love and of his abrupt refusal.

So what was she going to do now? Going back to Addie's and simply taking up where they'd left off seemed a complete impossibility. She'd never be able to look at him again. If she had felt mortified seven years ago, it was nothing compared to how she felt now. And he had had the nerve to say thank you! Her fingers itched to slap him. She had never met anyone else in her entire life who had had the power to make her want to curl up and die, and Jake Brosnan had done it twice!

She hadn't worn her swimsuit but she decided that it didn't matter. What mattered was forgetting this burning feeling that she'd had ever since he'd leapt out of bed and said, 'No.' Heedless of her corduroy shorts and navy T-shirt, she flung herself into the surf, swimming hard against the waves, needing to pit her strength against something elemental and indifferent, something that, if it hurt her, at least did so unintentionally. She swam parallel to the shoreline until she was exhausted. Her breathing came hard and racy, exertion forcing her to take short gasps; but still she ploughed on, wishing for an oblivion she hadn't wanted since she'd buried Paul.

She wanted to cry, and maybe she did. The tears and salt water were indistinguishable. But no relief came, no feeling of having washed away her troubles, only a mindless exhaustion that brought her up short. She was much too far out, the people on the beach were no bigger than sand fleas. No matter how she felt, the oblivion she sought wasn't the permanent sort. Get hold of yourself, she chastised herself firmly and turned shoreward. He's only a man.

Yes, she thought glumly, spitting out a mouthful of salt water, but he happens to be the man I love. *The man who doesn't love you*, a tiny inner voice taunted. But he does, she thought with a glimmer of insight. *I know he does.*

It was her first positive thought since she'd made her proposal of marriage, and it startled her so much she stopped stroking and promptly sank. Battling her way to the surface and shaking water from her eyes, she said it experimentally. 'He loves me.' The words felt strange. Foreign. 'He does,' she said with more conviction, tossing a strand of seaweed aside. Those were not only needs he had shown her last night. He had wanted her, yes, but there had been more to it than that. There had been a giving and a taking, sharing, loving. What had happened was not just the satisfaction of biological needs. It was a communing of spirits. Of souls.

Then why had he said no? Well, she admitted, it had been an awkward proposal. She hadn't had much experience at that sort of thing. And he had been half asleep. Maybe he needed time to think it over, to see how sensible and right their marriage would be.

Dream on, she chided herself sarcastically. But what was wrong with that? A little dreaming, a little perseverence might be just what she needed now. True, her first inclination had been to turn tail and run back to Galena. But now she knew she couldn't do that. She might be a fool for waiting, but who knew, maybe Jake Brosnan was one of the new breed of men, the ones who, like women, knew they had the prerogative to change their minds.

'I was afraid you were haring off back east,' Addie remarked when she came back.

'Why?' Torey looked up from where she was blow-drying her hair and met her grandmother's eyes.

'Because Jake's out there packing his truck looking like the God of Thunder himself. He says they're leaving for a spell. Going camping. I thought it might have something to do with you.' She looked at Torey as though she expected her granddaughter to explain.

Torey shrugged, feeling as though her horse had just been shot from beneath her. 'It might,' she said and set the drier down on the counter, went into her bedroom and closed the door. It was one thing for her to stand her ground and hope that Jake would come to his senses. It was another to realise that, even if she stood still, Jake might be the one to run. And what could she do about that? Nothing. Except hurt.

Her eyes lifted and she saw him thunder down the stairs carrying a sleeping bag and a box of kitchen gear. Oh Jake. Tears welled in her eyes and angrily she wiped them away.

Addie tapped lightly on the door. 'Going out to say goodbye?'

'No.' There was just so much rejection she could take. 'I think I'll take a nap,' she said, grateful that her grandmother couldn't see her red-rimmed eyes through the door. 'I—I didn't sleep much last night.'

But she lay cocooned not in slumber but in pain. Her ears heard every trip Jake made up and down the stairs; they heard Scott's high-pitched laugh and Jake's lower, gruffer tones. She twisted on the bed, covering her ears with the pillow, swallowing the ache in her throat. When the knock on the door came, it was so faint she nearly didn't hear.

'What is it?' she asked finally, sitting up and hastily drying her eyes. Didn't Addie ever give up?

'It's me.' Jake's voice was low and hesitant. 'I—I came to say goodbye.'

She rubbed the pillowcase over her face. 'Goodbye.'

The doorknob turned. She stared at it in panic. 'Torey?' He looked round the edge of the door, his deep-set eyes barely meeting hers before sliding away to stare instead at the picture of Paul.

'I said, goodbye.' It came out curt, almost angry. Good, she thought. I am angry.

Jake shoved his hands in his pockets and rocked back on his heels. 'I want to talk to you.' He shifted from one burgundy and grey running shoe to another and made fists with his hands, tautening the fabric of his jeans. She wished he hadn't—she didn't need any reminders of the shape of his body or the power of his lean, muscled thighs. 'I didn't mean for things to turn out like this,' he muttered at his toes. 'I do appreciate your offer. Er, I'm sorry.'

'I am too.' Her voice was cold, flat. He couldn't know how much she was hurting as she said it. She twisted the pillowcase in her hands. 'Thank you for coming.' She felt like the day she had listened to friends of Paul's come to offer their sympathies. There was nothing, absolutely nothing, she could say. 'Don't let me keep you, Jake,' she said finally, her eyes going pointedly to the door.

Jake pressed his lips into a thin grim line, then bowed his head. 'G'bye, Torey.'

The words hovered in the air long after she had heard the truck drive away.

The first really substantial snowfall came to Galena the night before Thanksgiving. It began as Torey finished helping her father with the milking, and the next morning it was still coming down. Even the weatherman was against her, Torey thought as she opened an eye and stared in dismay at the downy whiteness outside. She had endured a perfect autumn, ignoring leaves of flaming red and burnished gold, disliking crisp blue skies and Indian summer days. Only the bleak cold browns and greys of November touched a responsive chord in her, and now the sparkling snow eliminated even those. She groaned and pulled the scarf over her head.

If possible she felt worse this Thanksgiving than the one after Paul had died. Death, after all, was irrevocable. You accepted what you couldn't change and, however sadly, you went on. But Jake—how could she go on and forget Jake when he was still a living, breathing human being, still alive and still—God help her—loved?

She had tried, of course, to forget him. When she got back to Galena two days after he had left to go camping, she had thrown herself into every cause and job imaginable. She had gone to quilting bees and euchre parties, attended Octoberfests and church festivals, even accepting the occasional invitation from Harlan or Vince though she never let them kiss her goodnight. She also sent out scores of applications for jobs to big east coast cities. Her mother questioned her sanity, but Torey only replied, 'Last year you said I was vegetating,' and, as this was true, her mother pursed her lips in disapproval but made no more remarks.

Addie, of course, didn't help Torey's campaign to forget Jake. She wrote weekly to the family as a whole, but always with a postscript for Torey about the people she had met in California. For 'people', Torey thought, read 'Jake', for most concerned him. Nothing of a strictly personal nature, no testimonials about how gaunt and depressed he was, how much he pined for her to come back. Nothing that gave her that much satisfaction. Just reports on Scott in school, how Jake had finished the dragon book and was now working on another about a family with twelve children, how he had taken Scott to San Francisco. Just enough to whet her appetite, but never enough to make a meal on. The longer she was home, the more Torey was convinced that her grandmother had a sadistic streak.

What were they doing for Thanksgiving? Torey wondered. Would Addie and Jake share it? She grimaced thinking about the day in store for her here. She did not want to spend a day in the cheerful bosom of her family. It took too many muscles to smile for hours and hours. Maybe by Christmas she would have a job in Philadelphia or Boston. Somewhere far away from Christmas cheer. And a whole continent away from Jake Brosnan.

She dragged herself out of bed, already hearing her mother working at top speed in the kitchen preparing the turkey for the huge family gathering. Someone was chattering to her which meant that either one brother's family had arrived from Chicago or the other and his fiancée were there from Texas. Everyone else was going to be so happy and cheerful that she felt like a complete witch. She made an ugly face at herself in the mirror. Stop being so selfish and rotten, she told herself firmly. Do you think Jake is even thinking about *you* today? Forget Jake, she thought as she tucked in her navy and white gingham shirt and fastened her jeans. Today is not a day to be miserable. Today you should count your blessings.

Her blessings, in the form of an almost infinite number of relatives and friends, threatened to overwhelm her before the afternoon was over. The noise was unbearable, the joviality suffocating, and the heat from the oven enough to lay her flat out in a faint.

Her mother seemed all too aware of Torey's pallor. Even amidst her preparations of a salad for twenty-four she paused five times to inquire how Torey felt. 'Fine,' Torey lied with the regularity of an answering machine. But her mother looked at her sad face and deep-set shadowed eyes and shook her head. 'Open the olives, dear,' she said, handing Torey the cans, then turned to her sister-in-law, saying, 'Torey spent the summer in California, Madge.'

Aunt Madge took that as an excuse to talk about all the times she and Uncle Arnie had gone there, and Torey opened the olives and dumped them into a bowl, letting her aunt's relentless commentary wash over her. 'Movie studio,' Aunt Madge rabbited on. '. . . lines *that* long. Terrible smog, I told Arnie.'

'Oh heavens, I forgot,' Torey blurted, thrusting the dish of olives into her aunt's hand. 'Dad asked me to muck out the barn.' She made a dash for the door, shutting it behind her and leaning against it as if all the demons in hell were in pursuit.

Once the stinging cold had cleared her mind, mucking out the barn didn't seem like a half bad idea. If nothing else it suited her frame of mind. She slogged through the new fallen snow that clotted about her ankles, ignoring the small cousins pelting each other with snowballs, and slipped into the barn. Just as she did so she saw a late model silver car come round the bend in the gravel road. Just what she didn't need. It was probably Harlan, come to take her out for a spin in his new car. He had been threatening to buy one for the entire two months she had been home. Just last Monday he had settled on a particular Oldsmobile and had called to ask her out for a ride. She hadn't gone yet, and she was running out of excuses. Well, she thought with a giggle as she took down the shovel and headed for the biggest mess, he wouldn't want to take her today. Not when she smelled like this!

She began to shovel, the sheer physical labour gratifying her, but she was even more pleased when minutes passed and Harlan didn't appear. She stopped to rest for a moment, leaning on the shovel with her chin on her hands, and wondered where Jake was now. Stop it, she told herself. 'You're hopeless,' she muttered aloud, bending again to the task and hefting a particularly large shovelful of manure and tossing it in the direction of the door. It landed, she noted with consternation, on a pair of Etonic running shoes. Burgundy and grey running shoes. With feet in them. Jake's.

Stunned, her eyes ran rapidly up the legs of snug, well worn blue jeans past a navy down vest and soft red flannel shirt to settle on his lean, tanned face. It was every bit as gaunt and tired looking as she could have wished.

'I was hoping for a better welcome than that,' he said, a hesitant grin quirking up one corner of his mouth. 'But I guess it's the one I deserve.' He looked nervous and vulnerable with his hands shoved in the pockets of his vest and his head cocked to one side as he watched her with a mixture of emotions as complex as her own.

'Jake?' It was scarcely more than a whisper. She wanted to throw her arms around him, touch him, squeeze him, proving to herself that he was a real flesh-and-blood man and not the mirage she had been dreaming about for months. But her feet were lead, anchoring her to the soft dirt of the barn floor, and all she could do was stare.

'None other,' he agreed, the grin gentling into a sad smile as he stepped out of the manure and gingerly shook his feet one at a time. 'I thought,' he began slowly as he straightened up and faced her squarely, 'that you might like to know that you're not the only one grown-up enough to apologise.' His blue eyes were pleading, reaching out to her like rays of sun from the smudged, tired planes of his face. 'I'm sorry I acted like such an ass.'

'You——'

'Let me say it. God knows it's taken me long enough to get my life straightened out to where I finally felt I could come to you and actually do it.' He kicked at the

dirt, tracing a pattern in it with the toe of his shoe.
'You were right about letting Christy have a chance to
be with Scott. I did a lot of thinking while we were
camping. I needed to get things together. I didn't want
to marry you because I needed you for Scott.'

Torey's heart, which had leapt for joy at the sight of
him, abruptly crashed. He had come to apologise then,
nothing more.

'I didn't expect you to follow my line of thinking on
marriage so damned fast,' he said ruefully, raking
fingers through his hair. 'I didn't want to ask you to
marry me for the wrong reasons. And then,' he
shrugged helplessly, 'you did it for me.'

'I'm sorry,' Torey fumbled, unable to decide if she
felt more foolish or confused. What was he trying to
say?

'You're not supposed to apologise, damn it! I am!'
Jake growled, kicking one of the wooden uprights to
emphasise his frustration. He glared at her and, since
the only thing she could think to do was apologise
again, she wisely shut her mouth.

'I didn't know how to face you that morning,' he
said. 'I know I made a botch of it, but you gave me the
answer to all my problems but for the wrong reasons. I
thought you were offering to marry me out of pity. I
knew you already had a good marriage to Paul, so I
figured maybe you thought that this time you'd just do
a good deed—rescue poor old Jake from his folly——'

'Jake, I——'

'But I couldn't accept that. Not then. But when I
took Scott camping I began to wonder. I wanted to
come back and settle things with Christy before I came
to you again.'

'To me?' A ray of hope was dawning.

Jake shrugged. 'I was embarrassed. I didn't quite
know how I was going to work things out. But I
thought once I had, I could come back to you and
impress you with a *fait accompli*.' He grinned wryly.

'The trouble was, by the time the *fait* was *accompli*, you were long gone.

'I ironed things out with Christy,' he went on. 'I have custody of Scott, but he spends one weekend a month with them in San Francisco, also a couple of weeks during the summer. I sent him up there for a week in October—sort of a good faith gesture, I guess. Before he left I thought I would die of missing him. But the longer he was gone I realised that he wasn't the one I was missing. It was you, and I'd been missing you all along. I'm sorry.'

He stood like a statue then, his body as stiff and wooden as a cigar store Indian, waiting for her reaction. Only his eyes betrayed how uncertain he was.

Torey, always one to learn from past mistakes, flew to him, smiling like an angel as she tripped through the cow dung to throw her arms around him and whisper into his vest, 'It's all right, Jake. It's all right.'

He began to smile then, just slightly, as he bent his head, kissing her with a tenderness she had begun to think she had only imagined during all those weeks when he had been nothing more than a memory. Her fingers clenched on the soft cotton of his vest, digging into the down, proving beyond a doubt that he was real—hard, lean and warm against her.

As he lifted his lips away he smiled again, so wistfully it tugged at her heart. 'I know I can't ever be to you what Paul was,' he began carefully, his voice rough with emotion. 'I—understand that. But if you still want to marry me, I love you so much I'll take you any way I can get you.'

Torey lifted her eyes amazed. Had he finally said he loved her, after all? 'What?' she asked, wanting to be sure.

'I wanted you to marry me because of *me*, not Scott,' Jake said, his fingers biting into her woollen sweater. 'But I'll take you any way you'll come.'

'Jake,' she said softly, touching her fingers to his lips.

'I don't want another Paul. I loved him very much. But now I love you.'

It was Jake's turn to stare.

Torey laughed. 'Why did you think I proposed, Mr Brosnan? Certainly not because I felt sorry for you! I might have told myself that was why I was doing it, but really it was pure selfishness. I loved you and wanted to marry you. I thought it was a God-given opportunity to get what I wanted and to make things right for you at the same time.'

'Truly?' Jake was looking at her incredulously, a marvellous happiness dawning on his features. 'Oh Torey!' he muttered, his voice cracking as he hauled her against him, wrapping his arms around her so fiercely she thought she'd breathed her last. 'You really love me?' He took a step back, searching her face to be sure.

'Can't you tell?' Her fingers slipped beneath the vest to rove over his flannel shirt, loosening the buttons and tugged the shirt tails out of his jeans.

'I always knew you liked my body.' He grinned as his hands made similar explorations under her heavy Aran knit sweater. Callused fingers were undoing the buttons of her blouse, teasing her sensitive skin as they did their work.

'It was more than just your body,' she assured him, though there was no doubt that it was pretty wonderful too. 'It was your mind, your soul, every part of you. I was scared to death when I saw you in that airport. You were quite right about that.'

'Am I that frightening?' he chuckled, shivering under her touch.

'Definitely. The things you did to my pulses were not to be believed. I was used to a love like I'd felt for Paul. Calm, steadying, glowing. But with you it was lightning from the start. The moment I saw you again, after seven long years, it was like being hit with a brick.'

'You sure knew how to hit back,' Jake said drily. 'I thought you hated my guts, and frankly, remembering what you knew about me back then, I couldn't blame you if you did.'

'Oh, but . . .'

'No, really. Everything you said about me was right on the mark. Once I'd left college and the midwest behind, I was a different man. Wild doesn't begin to describe it. Every bit of sense my parents had pounded into me I gave up without another thought. God, was I an ass!' He shook his head and Torey saw pain in his eyes as he remembered. 'I guess it was Mick who made me see how destructive it was. After he died I grew up fast.'

'You weren't to blame for his death.' Torey threaded her fingers in his thick hair and kissed him, wanting to give him comfort.

'Not entirely,' he agreed, his breath warm on her cheek. 'But I had a part in it, and that's something I'll live with for the rest of my life. For a long time I think I put up with Christy's bitterness because it was like punishment for my guilt. But then I saw it was hurting Scott more than me. So when she said she wanted a divorce, I didn't fight it. I only wanted Scott and nothing else. At least until you came along.'

'And I was such a paragon of sweetness and light,' she mocked. 'Screaming at you, berating you, hurling abuse. It's a wonder you didn't strangle me instead of finally just getting mad and yelling back.'

Jake grinned. 'Your apology nearly knocked me off my feet. If you'd been Christy you'd have heaved a mug at me.' He touched the scar above his eye. 'That's what this was.'

Torey shrugged. 'Well, you were right. I *was* holding your past against you. I wanted to believe you were a rat. To defend myself, I guess. But after you so vividly called my attention to it, I had to think again. And what I thought was that you were tremendously attractive and maybe, just maybe, there was some reason for this incredible attraction I felt. So I decided to try and be friends. It was a start.'

'You make it sound like a biology experiment,' Jake teased, tormenting her breasts with his fingers so that she writhed against him. 'And what, may I ask were your results?'

Torey swallowed hard, wanting the delicious feelings to go on and on. 'I discovered that where there's lightning, there's fire! That day at the tidepools you nearly had me in flames.' Not to mention now, she thought.

'Me too. But coming home to find Christy quenched them fast enough.' He rested his cheek on her hair. 'I had wanted to ask you to marry me that day, to be the mother dragon in my life, but I was afraid it was too soon, what with Paul and such. Anyway, I thought we had lots of time. Then when Christy appeared I thought you'd interpret any proposal as just a means to keep Scott. I was afraid you'd think I was every bit as much a bastard as you'd imagined.'

'Not then,' Torey assured him. 'I knew I was falling in love with you then.'

'Well, I didn't,' Jake said. 'And besides, there was Gino.'

'Just a dear friend,' Torey smiled.

'He'd better be.' Jake's voice was ominous. 'He makes me jealous as hell. He was as right for you as I was wrong.'

'Not wrong, just unexpected. After Paul you weren't what I had in mind.' She grinned up at him, kissing the tip of his nose. 'I never wanted to fall in love with a man who had women scattered about littering up his life.'

Jake hooted with laughter. 'Women? What women? Where?' He looked around the empty barn in amusement.

'Lola?' It came out tentatively, but she had to say it.

'Lola?' Jake looked astonished. 'She's just a kid. The sort of kid you were seven years ago. She needs a keeper too. Her mother is a friend of mine's. You know what that's like.' He jerked his head towards the house, and Torey was reminded that his background of family and friends in Iowa were not unlike her own.

'That's all?'

'Of course.' He ruffled her hair.

'She spent the night with you.'

'In Scott's bed. Her roommates were having a wild party. I couldn't leave her there. You know what I'm like.' He grinned good-naturedly, and she poked him in the ribs, giggling,

'Ah yes. St Jake Brosnan, rescuer of damsels in distress.'

'Damn right,' Jake said. 'But I'm the one in distress right now, my love. What are we going to do about it?' He pressed her against his hips and she felt the extent of his distress.

'Oh Jake, there are twenty-three relatives in the house!'

'Twenty-five,' he said. 'I brought Addie and Scott. With so many there, they'd never miss us.'

'Want to bet? If my mother knew you were coming out here, she'd give us twenty minutes and send out a search party.'

'We can't roll in the hay?' he asked, burying his face in her hair.

'Not today.' She tugged on his head, turning it so that their lips met in a fiery kiss so hot and demanding that it shook her to her very core.

'My God, you set me on fire,' Jake rasped when they finally broke apart, dizzy and gasping, to stare into each other's eyes with joy.

'But of course,' Torey whispered. 'I'm a dragon.'

'You certainly are. My dragon.' He hugged her tightly, then tipped back his head and laughed.

'What's funny?' she asked, sliding her arm around his waist and hanging the shovel on the wall as she led him out the door.

'Just thinking about you taking inspiration from my

books.' Jake nestled her beneath his arm as he shut the door. They moved together through the gently falling snow towards the lighted house in the dim yard beyond. 'Wait'll you hear about the latest one.'

'What is it?' Torey's hip was hard against his, blue jeans brushing as they measured their steps through the wet, clinging snow.

'A picture book version of *Cheaper by the Dozen*!'

Twelve kids? Twelve! Torey's jaw dropped, and Jake, grinning, took immediate advantage of the situation, turning her in his arms and kissing her, the amusement giving way to passion in his face.

Naturally Torey kissed him back, noting just before she closed her eyes and surrendered to the love they shared that the white-haired old lady and the little blond boy, not to mention the twenty-three other people standing in the window watching them kiss, heaved one giant, collective sigh of relief.

Coming Next Month in Harlequin Presents!

847 LION OF DARKNESS Melinda Cross
The New York doctor, who's helped so many cope with blindness in a sighted world, is baffled by his latest case—and a force that threatens the doctor–patient relationship.

848 THE ARROGANT LOVER Flora Kidd
A young widow distrusts the man who tries to come between her and her Scottish inheritance. He made love to her, then left without a word nine years ago. Why should she trust him now?

849 GIVE ME THIS NIGHT Vanessa James
Passion flares between a tour guide and a mystery writer on the Greek island of Paxos. But she's blundered into his life at the worst possible moment—because around him, she senses danger!

850 EXORCISM Penny Jordan
Once she naively assumed he'd marry her if they made love. Now he wants her to help him research his new book in the Caribbean. Why? To exorcise the past?

851 SLEEPING DESIRE Charlotte Lamb
After a year apart, can an estranged wife forget the solicitor's letters and the divorce proceedings? Easily—when the man she loves reawakens her desire.

852 THE DEVIL'S PRICE Carole Mortimer
The day she left him, their love turned to ashes. But a London singer is willing to bargain with the devil to be with her lover again—but not as his wife!

853 SOUTH SEAS AFFAIR Kay Thorpe
Against her better judgment, against all her values, a young woman allows herself to be drawn into a passionate affair with her father's archenemy!

854 SUN LORD'S WOMAN Violet Winspear
Fate, which seemed to have been so kind, deals a cruel blow to a young woman on her wedding night, and her husband's desert kingdom loses its dreamlike appeal.

EYE OF THE STORM

MAURA SEGER

A powerful
portrayal of
the events of
World War II in the
Pacific, *Eye of the Storm* is a riveting story of how love
triumphs over hatred. In this, the first of a three-book
chronicle, Army nurse Maggie Lawrence meets Marine
Sgt. Anthony Gargano. Despite military regulations
against fraternization, they resolve to face together
whatever lies ahead.... Author Maura Seger, also known
to her fans as Laurel Winslow, Sara Jennings, Anne
MacNeil and Jenny Bates, was named 1984's
Most Versatile Romance Author by *The Romantic Times*.

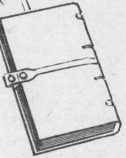

WORLDWIDE LIBRARY IS YOUR TICKET TO ROMANCE, ADVENTURE AND EXCITEMENT

Experience it all in these big, bold Bestsellers— Yours exclusively from WORLDWIDE LIBRARY WHILE QUANTITIES LAST

To receive these Bestsellers, complete the order form, detach and send together with your check or money order (include 75¢ postage and handling), payable to WORLDWIDE LIBRARY, to:

In the U.S.
WORLDWIDE LIBRARY
Box 52040
Phoenix, AZ
85072-2040

In Canada
WORLDWIDE LIBRARY
P.O. Box 2800, 5170 Yonge Street
Postal Station A, Willowdale, Ontario
M2N 6J3

Quant.	Title	Price
_____	ANTIGUA KISS, Anne Weale	$2.95
_____	WILD CONCERTO, Anne Mather	$2.95
_____	STORMSPELL, Anne Mather	$2.95
_____	A VIOLATION, Charlotte Lamb	$3.50
_____	LEGACY OF PASSION, Catherine Kay	$3.50
_____	SECRETS, Sheila Holland	$3.50
_____	SWEET MEMORIES, LaVyrle Spencer	$3.50
_____	FLORA, Anne Weale	$3.50
_____	SUMMER'S AWAKENING, Anne Weale	$3.50
_____	FINGER PRINTS, Barbara Delinsky	$3.50
	DREAMWEAVER,	
	Felicia Gallant/Rebecca Flanders	$3.50
_____	EYE OF THE STORM, Maura Seger	$3.50
_____	HIDDEN IN THE FLAME, Anne Mather	$3.50
	YOUR ORDER TOTAL	$_____
	New York and Arizona residents add appropriate sales tax	$_____
	Postage and Handling	$___.75
	I enclose	$_____

NAME _____

ADDRESS _____ APT.# _____

CITY _____

STATE/PROV. _____ ZIP/POSTAL CODE _____

WW2

The final book
in the trilogy by

MAURA SEGER

EDGE OF DAWN

The story of the Callahans and Garganos
concludes as Matthew and Tessa must stand
together against the forces that threaten to
destroy everything their families have built.

From the unrest and upheaval of the sixties
and seventies to the present, *Edge of Dawn*
explores a generation's coming of age
through the eyes of a man and a woman
determined to love no matter what the cost.

COMING IN FEBRUARY 1986

EDG-H-1

She fought for a bold future until she could no longer ignore the…

ECHO OF THUNDER

MAURA SEGER

Author of **Eye of the Storm**

ECHO OF THUNDER is the love story of James Callahan and Alexis Brockton, who forge a union that must withstand the pressures of their own desires and the challenge of building a new television empire.

Author Maura Seger's writing has been described by *Romantic Times* as having a "superb blend of historical perspective, exciting romance and a deep and abiding passion for the human soul."